CHILDREN IN
THE WIND

CHILDREN IN THE WIND

JÔJI TSUBOTA

Translated from the Japanese by

ROBERT EPP

LONDON AND NEW YORK

First published in 1991 by
Kegan Paul International

This edition first published in 2011 by
Routledge
2 Park Square, Milton Park, Abingdon, Oxfordshire OX14 4RN

Simultaneously published in the USA and Canada
by Routledge
711 Third Avenue, New York, NY 10017

First issued in paperback 2016

Routledge is an imprint of the Taylor and Francis Group, an informa business

British Library Cataloguing in Publication Data
A catalogue record for this book is available from the British Library

ISBN 13: 978-1-138-97036-6 (pbk)
ISBN 13: 978-0-7103-0393-6 (hbk)

Publisher's Note
The publisher has gone to great lengths to ensure the quality of this reprint
but points out that some imperfections in the original copies may be
apparent. The publisher has made every effort to contact original copyright
holders and would welcome correspondence from those they have been
unable to trace.

This translation is gratefully dedicated to

ROGER F. HACKETT

and

VAL H. VIGLIELMO

CHILDREN IN THE WIND

This novel was serialized in the evening edition of
the Tokyo *Asahi Newspaper* between September 5
and November 6, 1936; issued as a book in
December, 1936.

Scene: The summer of 1936 in the Japanese
countryside.

Cast of characters

SAMPEI AOYAMA (first grade, seven years old)
ZENTA AOYAMA (Sampei's big brother, fifth grade)
MRS AOYAMA (Sampei's mother)
ICHIRO AOYAMA (Sampei's father, manager of a
factory)

DR UKAI (Sampei's uncle, his mother's elder brother)
MRS UKAI (Sampei's aunt)
MIYOKO UKAI (Sampei's cousin; she is in the sixth
grade)
KOSUKE UKAI (Sampei's cousin; he is not yet in
school)

KINTARO (KIN) SAYAMA (second grade, Sampei's
friend)
MR SAYAMA (Kintaro's father)
JUZO AKAZAWA (supported Sayama against Sampei's
father)

GINJIRO (GIN)
TSURUKICHI   Sampei's friends
KAMEICHI

A policeman, a detective, a man from the court,
and a lawyer.

Pronunciation

Sampei = sam-pay; Aoyama = ah-oh-yah-mah;
Ichiro = ee-chee-roh; Ukai = oo-kah-ee;
Kameichi = kah-may-ee-chee.

Chapter One

The factory stood on the edge of the village. It employed forty people who made twine and ribbon. Though small, it was incorporated and its history reached back into the Meiji period. Its red brick chimney stuck proudly into the sky.

One summery day Sampei ran into Kintaro on the stone bridge by the factory. Sampei was in first grade, Kintaro in second. Kintaro had a chip on his shoulder and made fun of Sampei.

'What's the matter with you?' Sampei challenged. Kintaro continued to taunt him.

'What's the matter?' Sampei asked again, ready to fight. This time Kintaro answered haughtily, 'Your dad's gonna be fired.'

'No he's not,' Sampei said.

'Oh yes, he is. You'll see. They'll fire him and the cops'll come and take him away. They'll tie him up and haul him off, and he'll say "I'm sorry, forgive me, I won't do it again!"'

'Aw shut up.'

Sampei didn't want to hear any more. He picked up a stick and whacked Kintaro on the head. Then he threw the stick at Kintaro and ran toward home. After some sixty feet he looked back and saw Kintaro coming after him, his face purple with fury. Sampei impulsively picked up a stone from the road, threw it at Kintaro, and set off again. Thirty or forty feet before Sampei reached home he noticed his big brother standing by the gate. When Kintaro saw him he gave up the chase. After all, Zenta was a fifth grader.

'What's going on?' Zenta yelled at Kintaro.

'Well,' Kintaro shouted back, 'Sampei hit me on the head with a stick, and I didn't do anything to him. He gave me a real lump.' Kintaro put his hand to his head and made an appropriately painful expression.

'Liar!' cried Sampei, planting his left foot defiantly in front of him.

Zenta figured he was the one who should be scolding his little brother: 'Sampei, don't do things like that.'

'He's lying,' Sampei cried again.

'You mean you didn't just hit him with a stick?' Zenta asked. Kintaro took a step closer.

'Yeah, I hit him,' Sampei responded.

'Why did you do it?' Zenta asked. Sampei couldn't answer. He could only blink his eyes in protest.

Then Sampei also took a step forward and shouted, as though to explain why he had hit Kintaro, 'I hit him. Yeah, I hit him.'

By his words and the tone of his voice, Sampei meant to say that he had hit Kintaro for a good reason. But Zenta failed to get the message. He could only scold his brother: 'Sampei, you behave yourself.'

'Anyhow,' Sampei responded, 'it's Kin's fault.'

The moment he heard that, Kintaro jutted out his chin and said, 'What d'ya mean, my fault? Let's hear you explain that.'

Sampei couldn't explain what he meant. His cheeks reddened with rage. The words welled up in his throat but they simply refused to come out. He picked up another stone and stood with his arm extended, threatening to let it fly. Zenta got in front of him and held his arm: 'Cut it out! No rough stuff.'

'Awww . . . but it's Kin's fault,' Sampei said as he squirmed to get loose.

Chapter Two

While Zenta was trying to keep Sampei from throwing the stone, Kintaro cautiously retreated one step at a time. In this way he managed to preserve his dignity. When he was about sixty feet away he began taunting Sampei with a singsong:

Ha ha, you're stupid!
Your dad'll be arrested,
the cops'll tie him uuup –
then he'll say, 'I'm sorry,
I'll never do it again.'
Ha, haa, ha, ha!

With that he turned, took a skip and was off.

The brothers stood side by side, looking after him. Sampei still filled with spite, squeezed the stone all the harder. As Kintaro pranced about on the bridge again, Sampei took five or six spirited steps toward him and, though he couldn't possibly have scored a hit from that distance, let the stone fly with all his might.

When Kintaro was finally out of sight Sampei told his side of the story:

'Kintaro's a stinker,' he said.

'Why's he a stinker?' Zenta asked.

'Well, he . . .' Sampei dashed into the topic enthusiastically, but he choked up along the way; '. . . well, he says Daddy'll be fired and the cops'll take him away. But that won't happen, will it?'

''Course not.'

Despite his quick response, Zenta felt anxious about it. Shouldn't he tell his mother right away? He bobbed his head a few times as he considered what to do. When he was about to rush into the house Sampei asked, 'Zenta, where ya goin'?'

'Huh?' Sampei's question made him wonder. If he were to say

he's going in to tell his mother, wouldn't that sound childish? Wouldn't that be like a crybaby? Zenta caught himself. 'I'm just going to get something to drink.'

'Me too.'

The two of them scampered to where their mother was sewing. Zenta couldn't keep still about the incident. He blurted out, 'Mom, Kintaro Sayama has been teasing Sampei. He says Daddy'll be fired and taken away by the police.'

She looked up from her needlework but couldn't think of a response. It was unlikely that her husband had done anything wrong. Yet, the company had been in an uproar for some time, and stockholders are a crafty breed of people. If one of their children had predicted trouble, there probably would be trouble. No doubt some dark scheme was brewing. She recalled the dismal scandals that had occurred at the factory in the past. Her thoughts drifted off as she turned these events over and over in her mind.

Sampei noted her vacant stare and blurted out, 'But that's okay, Mom. I hit Kin with a stick for saying it. Pow! I really whacked him one. He says he's got a big lump on his head. And he was moaning and trying to keep from crying. I'll give him an even bigger lump if he says it again. And Mommy, if I do, he'll cry and say he's sorry. So its okay . . .'

'Do you think so?'

She didn't want to worry the children so she managed a bit of a smile. But she was uneasy and wanted to know more about the incident. 'What else did Kintaro say?'

'Nothing. If he did, I'd really have given it to him.'

Sampei was trying to talk big. Then he began worrying. What if his father found out? 'Mom, don't tell Daddy about the fight, okay? And don't say anything about the lump I put on Kintaro's head, either, all right?'

'All right, all right. But you should not get into fights!'

'Okay. If I do, though, I'm not gonna get beat.' Sampei felt relieved, but he was still talking big.

Chapter Three

Summer vacation came. Suddenly it seemed as though the village children had multiplied. You could hear their voices wherever you went.

Sampei set out as usual to meet his father. Soon the factory would have its three-o'clock break – time for Daddy to bring him a treat from the company store.

But for some reason or another a number of boys had gathered at the factory gate. A general meeting of the stockholders had been called. It was the day for hatching plots to topple Sampei's father, Mr Aoyama, from his position as an executive in the company. It was the day Kintaro's father, Mr Sayama, would take over the vacated position. Of course, Sampei was not aware of such plots.

'Hi!' he called as he ran over to the others. All his friends were there – Kintaro, Ginjiro, Tsurukichi, and Kameichi. Today, however, not a one responded to his greeting. They pretended not to hear him.

'Hey, what's up?' He was sporting a big smile. They remained silent. Sampei wondered what on earth was happening. 'Maybe it's because of the fight', he thought, so he asked Kintaro directly: 'Hey, Kin, you mad at me?'

'Naw,' Kintaro said, shaking his head.

'Oh . . . ? Then let's play.'

'Okay.'

Relieved, Sampei wedged himself into the group. At that moment a man dressed in his Sunday best walked through the factory gate.

'Number five,' Kintaro called out.

'He's number six,' said Ginjiro.

'No, he's five,' Kintaro insisted.

'He's number five, just like Kin says,' Kameichi asserted,

fawning on Kintaro. They were counting the men who showed up for the stockholders' meeting. Sampei looked on, blissfully unaware that these men would vote his father out of his position and suggest that Kintaro's father take his place.

'Why count 'em?' Sampei asked.

Nobody answered. More stockholders arrived.

'Number six, number seven, number eight,' Kintaro shouted. The three men smiled at Kintaro. One said, 'Well, well, you're gatemen, are you? Doing a fine job.'

So that's it, playing gateman. Now Sampei thought he had figured it out. Maybe there was some sort of celebration at the factory today. He'd try to do a fine job, too. When Sampei saw a group of four men approaching, he was the first to cry out, 'Number nine, number ten, number eleven, number twelve.' The four stopped talking when they heard Sampei's voice. They glared at him. He felt a bit uneasy.

Sampei wondered whether he had perhaps gone too far. Would he be scolded if he stayed? He was not the kind of boy to flinch at anything, so when he saw the next group of men coming to the meeting he yelled, 'Thirteen, fourteen, number fifteen.'

In this group was Juzo Akazawa, one of the directors of the company. Sampei hoped for a smile of recognition. Instead, Akazawa stopped in front of Kintaro, hunched down a little and asked, 'Are most of them here?'

'Just fifteen so far. But Sampei's being a pest.'

'Ignore him. He doesn't understand.'

Sampei couldn't bear to let that pass. 'I do too.'

'Say, you're pretty clever, young man.'

'You bet.'

Akazawa forced a sour smile and went into the factory. That's what Sampei had been hoping for. He suddenly felt cheerful again.

Chapter Four

The boys had been waiting by the gate for some time when Kintaro came running out of the building. 'Hey, go look. They're having a fight in the office. Sampei's dad is arguing like mad with everybody.'

They took off like lightning. The workers, both men and women, had lined up outside the office, straining to hear what was happening. The boys broke through the line and climbed like monkeys up the barred windows of the company office. Sampei, right with them, peered inside. At that moment a flood of people spilled out of the office building. The meeting had ended. Buzzing noisily, most headed for the gate, though a few went into the factory. When Akazawa came out, a number of factory hands abruptly returned to their work.

Kintaro spotted his father among those on their way out of the gate. 'Dad! How about some caramels,' he wheedled.

'Not now.'

'Aw, come on.'

By the time Sampei became aware of what was happening, everybody had gone. The only one he could see in the room was his father, sitting alone at his desk, puffing his cigarette like a smoke stack. Sampei went into the office and ran over to him, 'Daddy!'

No answer. His father continued staring.

'Come on Dad, let's go home.'

Sampei laid his arm across the back of the chair and looked into his father's big eyes. He saw no response. His father didn't seem aware of his presence. Then the boy shouted loudly, right into his father's ear, 'Daddy, I've been waiting a long time for you. You didn't come out at three today. Now it's five already.'

No response. Sampei took the lid off his father's writing box and began to play with the pens and the seals in it. After a while he asked, 'Dad, did you fight with them, huh? Did you win?'

A secretary entered and Sampei's father finally spoke. 'Where is everyone?' he asked.

'The clerks and factory hands are in the dining hall listening to what Mr Sayama has to say,' she answered.

'Oh, are they? I'd like to say something to them, too, but I can do that tomorrow. We'll arrange for Sayama to take over then. Please tell him that for me, won't you?'

Sampei's father got up. That made Sampei happy because he was impatient to leave. Standing next to the desk, he clung to his father's hand. As they were about to step down into the en- tranceway, Sampei realized that his father still had his slippers on. 'Dad, how about your shoes?'

Sampei went to get the shoes. He knew where everything was because he met his father every day. Then he thought of the hat, walked over to the hat rack and jumped up to get it. 'Have you forgotten anything else, Daddy?' he asked. He often said such precocious things.

He took his father's hand and the two of them headed for the gate. Sampei really beamed whenever he walked with his father. Not even a dog could frighten him then. And as for kids from other villages – he could take on any number of them!

Sampei didn't say another word until, after leaving the factory gate, they had turned the corner. 'Dad, did you quit? . . . Well, you don't need this old factory. You can just build your own.'

As they approached the house, Sampei ran ahead and shouted in from the front door, 'Mommy, Daddy's home! He quit his job. He says he's going to build a new factory.'

Chapter Five

Sticking out above the green of the lush persimmon tree was a small rising-sun flag. It fluttered in the breeze. Zenta had just attached it to the top of the tree. Sampei was standing below, watching.

'Hey, Zenta, can you see far from up there?'

'Yep.'

'Can you even see Mount Fuji?'

'Yep.'

'Is it snowing there?'

'Yep.'

'Is the wind blowing?'

'Yep.'

'Gosh! Are you going to stay up there a while?'

'Yep.'

Zenta's answers did not really satisfy Sampei, but he was happy just the same.

He wanted so much to climb the tree by himself. He wrapped both arms and legs around the thick trunk. Before he had shinnied up a foot, however, he slipped back down. Next he spit on his hands and energetically leapt at the tree. Alas, he slid down again. What could he do but call up to his brother for more information?

'Zenta, can you see the ocean from there?'

'Yep.'

'Are there any steamers on it?'

'Yep.'

'Can you see any whales swimming around?'

'Yep.'

'Gee, how about a whaler?'

'Natch!'

'Holy cats! . . . They catching any whales?'

'Yep, they are.'

Just then Zenta slid like grease from his perch. He had seen Kintaro, Tsurukichi, and a few other neighborhood boys. 'Say, Sampei, let's go catch some fish and bugs. And bring back a crab, too.'

'What for?' Sampei didn't feel right about it. Anyhow, the flag had just been hoisted, hadn't it? How could they go out bug catching without singing a song or blowing a bugle? Wasn't there a rule about that somewhere?

But Zenta said, 'We'll catch locusts and beetles, and then a frog and a carp. Okay? We'll set up a Great Big-Game Kingdom. Zenta and Sampei'll be president. You've seen *Tarzan of the Apes*, haven't you? In the movie he had elephants and hippos working for him, and he did great things, remember? Come on, we'll try it too.'

That would be fine indeed. Sampei jumped up with joy. 'Okay, let's go,' he said. They ran to the shed to get out a bamboo fish basket and their insect net. Sampei held the basket, Zenta the net. They stood in ranks before the gate with pieces of bamboo stuck into their belts to serve as swords or rifles for taking big game.

''Tenn-shun! Forward, march!'

They lifted their knees high, swung their arms, and marched off. They had also dropped the straps on their school caps and pulled them tightly under their chins because this was a crisis. It was only yesterday that their father had lost his job. Today the two of them must stand together and guard their home against Kintaro and the rest. They had their own little world to defend.

Zenta, spying an insect in the grass by the path, commanded himself: 'A grasshopper. Capture the monster!' He netted it nimbly.

'Hey, Zenta! A frog. A king frog. Take 'im,' Sampei ordered. Zenta scooped him up. Twenty or thirty minutes of marching resulted in a clamor of buzzing and whirring inside the basket. Added to the grasshopper and the king frog were a locust, a carp, a beetle, and a stag beetle.

The boys lustily sang the Waseda University song as they returned in triumph from their campaign.

Chapter Six

The little rising-sun flag attached to the tip of the persimmon tree trembled in the morning breeze. Zenta, his head sticking out of the leaves next to the flag, shaded his eyes from the morning sun and gazed into the distance. Sampei stood underneath, asking questions again.

'Zenta, can you still see Mount Fuji from up there?'

'Yep, I can see it.'

'And is it snowing on top?'

'Yep, it's snowing.'

At that moment Zenta spotted a man in a white uniform standing on the stone bridge by the factory. A sword dangled at his side. Zenta no sooner thought, 'A cop!' than the man turned and began walking toward their house. 'What can we do? I'm sure he's coming to take our dad away.'

'Zenta, can you see the ocean?'

Zenta was too alarmed to answer. His legs and his arms trembled . . . 'Oh, don't let the policeman come to our house!' Zenta shut his eyes and clasped his hands in front of him. 'It'd be great,' he thought, 'if only I could use some magic now. I'd change the policeman into a grasshopper, just like that, and chase him into the field.' Why not try it? Zenta started praying fervently: 'God, let me work magic on him, let me work it . . .'

Sampei didn't know what was happening, so he continued asking for information. He shouted to his brother, 'Hey Zenta, what's up? Are they catching whales now?'

Meanwhile Zenta was peeking down the road through his half-closed eyes. Yes, the policeman was still coming his way. In a twinkling, Zenta made up his mind. He was determined to rely on the magic. God would certainly help him.

'Oh, God,' he had meant to say – his eyes shut, his face turned up, his body bent back. But all that came out was a garbled shriek as he slipped and fell over backward.

Sampei was shouting from the ground, 'Zenta! Zenta!'

Whether the prayer had been answered or whether the magic had worked, one thing was sure. Somebody was looking after Zenta. A branch under him broke his fall and supported his entire weight.

The policeman in his white summer uniform had stopped in front of the house. Sampei finally became aware of him. 'Gosh, a cop!' he cried as he ran to block the gate. He got there at precisely the right moment to prevent the officer from opening it.

'Hey, what are you trying to do?' asked the policeman.

'You can't come in here,' Sampei said heroically.

'Why can't I?'

Sampei didn't answer. He merely continued pushing at the gate for all he was worth, groaning under the strain.

'Well, how do you like that?' the officer said. Then he began pounding on the gate. Sampei could not prevent that.

'Hello there, anybody home?'

Sampei's mother came out. 'Yes, what is it? ... my, my, Sampei, what are you doing?'

'Haha, it looks like he's done something bad,' the officer chuckled as he walked through the gate, notebook in hand. He was visiting the homes on his beat to make a routine head count. 'Family of four – no changes?' he asked. Then he left.

After the officer had gone, Sampei went over to the persimmon tree again and shouted up to his brother, 'Zenta, aren't they shooting off fireworks some place? Can't you hear any fireworks?'

The policeman had left without causing any trouble. The morning breeze quivered the flag. Zenta slid down the tree. Both he and Sampei were delighted with the way things had turned out. They felt like doing something.

Chapter Seven

'Zenta, how about a game?'

'Okay.'

'Great!' Sampei had thought of something terrific. He went to the shed and brought out a length of straw matting. He laid it out under the persimmon tree.

'Zenta, how about Olympics?'

'Okay.'

'You announce it, I'll swim.' Sampei stretched out on his belly ready to begin swimming on the mat. 'C'mon, Zenta, let's go.'

Zenta sat on top of an empty five-gallon oil can he had brought up and, with both hands to his mouth, made a megaphone.

'Ready?'

Zenta started. 'This is an Olympic swimming competition. In the first lane is Sampei.'

'That's no good. You got to say it louder.'

To accommodate Sampei, Zenta raised his voice. 'In lane two is Hamuro*, in lane three, Tajima. In lane four, Maehata, in lane five a Frenchman, in lane six an Englishman . . .'

Sampei had already stretched out his arms and legs on the mat, assuming the attitude of a swimmer.

'They're on their marks. And there's the gun! They're off. They're in the water. They're still under. Haven't surfaced yet. (Hey, Sampei, you just dove in. C'mon, you're still under water.)'

Sampei, who had been thrashing his arms and legs wildly, took a cue from the announcer, put his head on the mat, and began stroking like a frog through the water.

*Some of the humor of this passage depends on knowing the identity of the people Zenta mentions. Each took a gold medal in the 1936 Berlin Olympics: Tetsuo Hamuro in the men's 200-meter breast stroke, Naoto Tajima in the triple jump, Hideko Maehata in the women's 200-meter breast stroke.

'Now they're up. They've surfaced. Sampei's in front. Hamuro's second. It looks like a two-man race. (Sampei, you're not under water any more. Come on, get those arms and legs moving!) Sampei's in the lead now. He's ahead. Hamuro's dropped back. One meter. Two meters. He's already five meters behind. Now, the fifty-meter mark. Sampei turns. (Come on, Sampei, face the other way.)'

The announcer was quite busy. And Sampei was swimming in dead earnest. He spun around on his belly and continued flapping his arms and legs like a windmill.

'Tajima was way behind, but he just took a hop, step, and jump. Now he's in the lead.'

Sampei stopped swimming and looked up at his big brother. 'Come on Zenta. What're ya talking about, he "took a hop, step, and jump"?'

'Never mind. You're supposed to be in a race now. If you ask questions like that you'll get behind.'

Sampei turned his attention back to the race, swimming with powerful strokes – now on his back, now on his belly – as he rolled around the mat.

'Look, Maehata's come up. Sampei has dropped back to last place!'

'Aw, cut it out,' Sampei said, raising his head from the mat again, 'I don't like to be last.'

'Okay, okay. So you're first. Sampei's in first place, he's taken the lead. Hamuro's second, Maehata third, Tajima fourth. The Frenchman and the Englishman are fifth and sixth. But they're all very close. It's a tight spot for Sampei. He may still come in last. Now it looks like the Frenchman may be first. Come on Sampei, give it all you've got. Hold on, hold on!'

At that point Sampei put on a terrific spurt. His face was up, then it was down. He beat the mat with his arms. He kicked it with his feet. He even turned somersaults on it.

'He won, he won! Sampei won!'

Sampei stretched out on the mat, drenched in sweat.

Chapter Eight

It was almost lunch time. Sampei got on his tricycle and rode off
to the bridge by the factory. On the way, a man riding a bicycle
came toward him, ringing his bell. Not to be outdone, Sampei
tinkled his bell, too.

The man got off his bike, brimming with smiles, and asked
Sampei, 'Hi there! Do you know where Ichiro Aoyama
lives?'

'Sure.'

'Where?'

'In our house.'

'Oh, in your house, really? Well, how about showing me the
way?'

Sampei proudly pedaled his trike ahead of the man, jingling
his bell occasionally though nobody was in the way. When he
came to the corner he gave a turn signal, and when they arrived at
the gate he commanded, 'Halt!'

He shouted into the entranceway, 'Somebody's here,
Mommy, somebody's here.'

The man smiled at Sampei as he asked, 'Say, how old are you?'

'Seven.'

'Well then, you're in first grade, right? Or is it second?'

'First.'

'My, a first grader. That's something.'

The moment Mrs Aoyama came to the door the man became
serious. He took a calling card from his pocket and asked, before
giving it to her, 'Is your husband home?'

'Yes, he is.'

'He's here now, then?'

'Yes, he is.'

'Well, I'd like to see him if I may.'

With that he handed her the card. While Mrs Aoyama stared

at it, he gradually pulled in his chin and looked down, fixing his
eyes somewhere on the ground before him.

'Mr Aoyama *is* home, isn't he?'

'Yes, he's home.'

'Well, I'd like to get going, so if you don't mind . . .'

Mrs Aoyama went to fetch her husband. She had turned pale.
Sampei was afraid this fellow had come to threaten his father. He
feared that his father might come out shouting. But his curiosity
soon got the better of his fears.

'Where you from, Mister?' The man didn't answer. He looked
intently into the house.

Sampei asked again, 'What do you want, Mister?' The man,
paying no attention to Sampei, called directly into the house: 'He
is in, isn't he? I'd like him to come out for a moment.'

Mr Aoyama came out.

'You're Mr Aoyama, aren't you?'

'That's right.'

'Ichiro Aoyama, correct?'

'That's correct.'

'Well then, could you come to the station with me?'

'What do they want with me?'

'Actually, I'm not sure. But it's just a formality. You can settle
it in a jiffy.'

'Do you think so? If it'll take some time, I should make a few
arrangements . . .'

'Oh no, it'll only take a minute. I'm sure it's nothing at all.'

Looking concerned, Mr Aoyama slipped into some clogs and
went along without changing his clothes. His wife stood silently
in the entranceway, gazing after him.

Sampei and Zenta watched these strange going-on from where
they stood near the gate. Their father walked ahead along the
river road that led to town. The man from the police station
followed him, pushing his bike.

After the two turned out of sight, Zenta and Sampei dashed
over to their mother and asked, 'Who's that man, Mom? What
did he want?' Mother didn't answer. She just stood there with a
lost look on her face.

Chapter Nine

It was one o'clock already, well past lunch time. Both Zenta and Sampei were starved. Rather than go inside, however, they went under the persimmon tree and sat on the oil can Zenta had used when he announced the Olympics. After Father left with the man from the police station, Mother stood bracing herself momentarily against the inside door at the entranceway.

When Sampei glanced at the doorway a little later, she was no longer there. He was eager to go into the house, for he had a thousand questions to ask her. Zenta had prevented that by grabbing his shoulders, leading him to the persimmon tree, and sitting him down on the oil can.

An hour had passed. They were dying of hunger and Sampei wanted ever so much to shout at the top of his lungs, 'Mom, is lunch ready yet?'

Zenta wouldn't let him. He sensed his mother's predicament and, wishing to leave her alone, was trying to divert his little brother's attention.

'Sampei, what would you like more than anything in the whole world?'

'I want some lunch.'

'C'mon, I'm not talking about lunch.'

'Well, a snack would be okay, too.'

'I'm not talking about a snack either. I don't mean food.'

'Okay, money.'

'Cut it out. I don't mean anything like that.'

'Well, what's left?'

'You're impossible! I'll tell you what I want more than any-thing – a lamp.'

'A lamp? A lamp for your bike?'

'For cryin' out loud, not a lamp for a bike!'

Then Zenta told his brother about Aladdin's magic lamp and

the tale of the Arabian Nights. 'How about that, eh? You just rub the lamp a little and the genie stands before you. 'Yes, Master, I am the genie of the lamp, at your command.' That's what genies say. 'Bring me some bread,' you say, and in a flash, right before your eyes is a big loaf – fluffy fresh – right out of the oven.'

When he heard that, Sampei unconsciously swallowed hard. 'Gee!' He was impressed. He cocked his head to one side, lost in thought for a moment. Then he asked, 'Do they still have lamps like that?'

'They might. Then again, they might not.'

'Boy, oh boy, it'd be great to have one.' But Sampei was too famished to get interested in genies. 'Dog-gone, I'm starved!' The more he said it the hungrier he got. He couldn't sit still a moment longer. Noticing a stick lying under the persimmon tree, he flew off to pick it up.

'Hey, persimmon Aladdin,' he yelled at the tree, walloping the trunk with his stick, 'bring me some food. I'm starved. Bring me something good, some *sushi* or bean-jam buns.'

He whacked the tree again with all his might. When Zenta saw his brother hitting the tree, he suddenly forgot how bad he felt. 'Okay, now let me try it too.' He came up with a stick of his own and laid a blow on the persimmon tree. 'Say, you Aladdin's persimmon lamp, you genie of the lamp, bring me a bun. Get me some sponge cake.'

The two of them mercilessly thumped the persimmon tree. But that was not enough to satisfy them. 'Zenta, how about trying it on the pine out front?'

'Okay.'

From the pine they turned their attention to the loquat tree, and from the loquat to the cypress. They were hoping they might hit on the right tree, the tree with magic, from which a real genie would emerge.

'Hey, genie of the cypress, bring us five new factories.'

While shouting this new silliness, they were relieved to hear their mother call, 'Lunch time!'

Chapter Ten

Both Zenta and Sampei had gone to bed. They weren't really sleeping – they just pretended they were. Mother was still up. She was waiting for Daddy to return.

It got later and later. The boys couldn't hear a sound outside. It was pitch dark all over the world. And still Father had not returned. They wondered what had happened to him. Had he been tied up by the police? Had he been put into jail?

Mrs Aoyama imagined him bound and behind bars. But she kept busy as a bee with her sewing. Without something like that to do, she couldn't possibly have sat still. She listened intently for any noises outside the house. At each sound she wondered, 'Was that a footstep? Was that somebody clearing his throat out there?'

Just then Sampei clattered out of bed and went to the front door.

'Is that you, Sampei?' she asked.

'Yep.'

'Where are you going?'

'Wee-wee.'

'Wee-wee? But you're at the front door.'

'Yep.' Sampei had already stepped down into the entranceway and opened the door.

'Where are you going?' She stood up, somewhat concerned.

'Oh, I'm going to the toilet outside.'

Sampei went to the bathroom just outside the gate. He didn't come back into the house right away. He stood there thinking: 'They'll come from beyond the factory. No, from town. That's right.' He was staring down the road that led to the police station. He, too, was waiting for Father to come home.

'Sampei, what are you doing out there?'

'Looking at the stars.'

'Quit fooling around and come back inside,' his mother's voice demanded.

'Okay. I'm looking for a falling star.'

It was only after giving this excuse that he actually looked up into the sky. Lots of stars were twinkling away up there. The glittering lights of the night sky stretched to the ends of the earth. Sampei imagined his father wearily trudging along somewhere under that endless sky.

'Aw, no stars are falling.'

Nevertheless, he didn't budge.

'Come in right this minute,' his mother's voice commanded.

'Okay.'

Off toward the road it was very dark. He strained his ears in that direction. Were those footsteps? When he realized they were not, he went back into the house.

'It's dark out there. I didn't see one shooting star.' The moment he got back into bed, he realized he was too wide awake to sleep. 'I don't feel like sleeping now,' he said as he plopped down next to his mother.

Zenta also got up and came into the room. His excuse was, 'It's too hot to sleep.'

By that time, Mrs Aoyama hardly cared. She had completely lost the power to concentrate. She didn't know what to think. Nor did she know where to find out what had happened to her husband. The police station was far away, and there was no one to whom she could turn for help.

'I'm going to the toilet,' Zenta announced as he went out the front door.

Sampei got up to follow. 'I feel like going again too,' he said. They met by the gate.

'Zenta, how about walking over to the other side of the factory?'

'Okay, let's go.'

They held hands. Sampei felt like singing, so he started to blurt out the Keio University song. 'Knock it off!' Zenta said. He didn't want to let anybody know they were coming.

Chapter Eleven

'Time to get up, boys. After breakfast, Mother's going to get Daddy.'

Mrs Aoyama was in great spirits this morning. She hadn't slept a wink all night, worrying about what to do. But she had finally decided that this was no time for tears. Of course the children knew nothing of her decision. They happily jumped out of bed and raced to see who could wash up faster. When they got to the table Sampei said, 'Bring me back a present from town.'

'Well, now, can you boys behave yourselves and watch the house while I'm gone? No matter who comes, say nobody's home and don't let them through the front gate.'

After she left, they shut the gate, closed the hasp and stuck a nail in it. They tugged with all their might to see if they could open it. When they were sure it was secure, they went into the living room and sprawled out on the floor. Assured the house was safe, Sampei felt so relieved that the sandman suddenly began to bother him.

'Zenta, how about taking a nap?'

'I'm not sleepy,' Zenta said. He just felt depressed.

'If we nap, Dad and Mom might come home. They'll have presents for us from town,' Sampei said.

'Right,' Zenta said. 'But I'm not sleepy.'

Sampei shut his eyes. In a moment he was fast asleep and snoring lightly, for he had slept very little the night before.

He must have napped for an hour. When he awoke he found Zenta stretched out beside him, blinking his eyes.

'Zenta, aren't you sleepy?'

'Nope.'

'If you can't get to sleep I can sing you a lullaby. How about it?'

'Don't be silly,' Zenta snapped. As he lay on his side fat tears rolled down his cheeks. He had been thinking about things for a long time. Sampei, not realizing what Zenta was doing, started jabbering again.

'How about telling stories, Zenta?'

'No thanks.'

'Come on, let's talk about something.'

'I don't want to. That's no fun.'

'It is too. I can tell fairy tales, like Momotaro or the sparrow with the cut tongue.'

Since Zenta didn't respond, Sampei went right on. 'Say, Zenta, listen. I'll tell you one, okay? Once upon a time there was this sparrow with a cut tongue, and ...'

'Shut up. Who believes that sort of ...'

Rapping at the front gate! 'Oh boy, it's Daddy,' Sampei said as he jumped up. Zenta quickly caught him before he started to dash outside. 'No it isn't, that's for sure.' They strained their ears and heard a voice call, 'Mr Aoyama, are you home?'

Sampei looked up at Zenta as if to ask, 'What shall we do?'

Zenta kept hold of Sampei. The voice became louder, the rapping on the gate more furious. 'Mr Aoyama, are you in? Isn't anybody home? If you don't answer, I'll climb over the fence.'

The voice belonged to Juzo Akazawa from the factory. Sampei couldn't contain himself and wriggled for all he was worth to escape Zenta's grip. Then the voice said, 'What shall we do? How about getting an officer as a witness?'

'It'll take too much time to do that. Let's wait until tomorrow morning.'

Another man was with Mr Akazawa. The two voices trailed off as the men left.

'Safe!'

The boys nodded at each other in relief. After listening carefully for a while, they smiled happily. Of course, they had no way of knowing that the man with Akazawa had come from the court to seize their property.

Unconcerned, Sampei picked up Mother's yardstick, assumed the posture of a swordsman ready to do battle, and put on a fierce face. 'Yaaa! Nobody's home today. Heeeey! Mom and Dad are gone.' He slashed about to scatter the enemy. After the battle, Sampei went through the warrior's suicide ritual and slumped over dead. It was an honorable way to go.

Chapter Twelve

They waited and waited for Mother to come home with Daddy, but she didn't show up. As they waited they talked things over in front of the alarm clock. It was exactly two o'clock when Zenta said, 'I bet they'll be home when the little hand comes to here,' pointing to three.

Sampei said, 'I bet they'll be back when the big hand comes to here,' pointing to two.

'Are you serious? That's only ten minutes from now,' Zenta said.

'That's right. There's a whole ten minutes.' Sampei was determined to stick by his statement.

'So if the big hand comes to two and they're not back yet, then what?'

'Anything you want,' Sampei said.

'I get your knife?'

'Sure, you can have it.'

They began their vigil, perched in front of the clock. Sampei kept saying, 'Hurry back, hurry on back. Dad and Mom, Mom and Dad, hurry back.'

Before he knew it, the big hand had moved five minutes.

Zenta kept saying, 'Take your time, take your time, it's okay to take your time. Mom and Dad, Dad and Mom, take your time.'

When the big hand was two minutes short of pointing to ten past two, Sampei suggested a change: 'I'll make it the next time the big hand comes to two.'

'That's cheating,' Zenta protested.

'Why not when the hand comes around once? Zenta, it's okay with me if you change yours too – till the small hand comes to three again.'

Things were fairly well mixed up by now. The big hand pointed to two each hour, but the small hand would not pass three again for another twelve hours.

'No, you don't. I won't go along with that. I won, so I get your knife. Okay? Look, your hand is already at two,' said Zenta, pointing to the big hand. He stood up to go get the knife.

Sampei, trying to detain him, whispered, 'Zenta, somebody just called me.'

'They did?'

The two of them looked around. Zenta thought mainly about keeping cool in such instances.

'You're kidding me,' he said.

They grasped each other's hands and strained their ears. 'See,' Zenta said knowingly, 'nobody's there.'

'I thought I heard someone,' Sampei said, cocking his head.

Zenta called, 'Who's there? Who called "Sampei"? Who is it? . . . See, just like I said. Nobody there.' But as he said it, Zenta was quaking.

Then, in a voice purposely bold, Zenta bravely headed into the next room. 'Let's go around and see. Maybe it was a stray dog. Scat, you!'

Sampei, feeling quite cocky after that, scooted into the living room as he yelled loudly, 'Scat, kitty!'

He ended up in the bathroom, shouting ridiculously: 'Why did you call "Sampei"? Hey, are you going to say it again, huh? Just try it! Come on. The cat got your tongue?' He tried his best to impress Zenta with his boldness.

Despite the ruckus, the eerie feeling of loneliness that fell over the house remained. Mother did not return that night.

Chapter Thirteen

Uncle Ukai had a handlebar mustache so long you could see it from behind. He was Mrs Aoyama's big brother. Long ago he had been an army surgeon, but now he practiced medicine in a small village some twelve or so miles back in the hills. Yesterday Mrs Aoyama had gone to fetch him.

'Well, now, there's nothing to worry about,' Uncle Ukai said. 'If your father doesn't come back, you can all stay at my place. We have birds in our hills and fish in our streams. You won't get bored, though we're off the beaten track.'

Zenta and Sampei were in a good mood that morning. Their uncle's hearty laugh had helped cheer them up. Just after finishing breakfast they heard – amid a peal of laughter – someone opening the front gate.

A voice called out, 'Hello . . .'

Two men stood in the entranceway. They were Juzo Akazawa from the factory and the man from the court, the same two who had pounded on the locked gate the day before. Tension mounted when it became clear who the men were.

'We're coming in,' Akazawa announced boldly. He entered the living room with the other man right on his heels.

'Go outside and play,' Mrs Aoyama said to the boys. Zenta and Sampei were as apprehensive as they were curious about what was happening. But they had no choice, so they went outside and stood under the persimmon tree. The brothers were too upset to ask each other what this might mean.

Zenta climbed to the top of the tree; Sampei stood underneath, getting angrier by the minute. He was in a terrible mood.

If only there had been a huge boulder nearby, he would have pushed it with all his might and turned it over. Even one big as a house. There was no boulder. Instead Sampei decided he would climb the persimmon tree. He wrapped his arms and legs around it and grunted as he tried to shinny up the trunk. He edged up about a foot. Each time he tried to pull his legs up to where the rest of him was, he slipped back down again.

'I'm gonna make it this time.'

He even pressed his cheek hard against the trunk. But every time he shinnied up he slid back down. And every time he slid down he scraped his cheek on the bark. Soon his face was a mass of white scratches. In his mood the smart from his scratches actually felt good.

Suddenly he realized that he had made at least a dozen attempts to shinny up the tree, yet he was still sitting flat on the ground.

He was furious by now. 'Come on you!'

He stripped off his shirt. He was already barefoot and in his shorts. He spit into his hands and rubbed some sticky dirt on his legs. Then he walked thirty or forty feet from the tree and sprinted back toward it. At the right moment he jumped, springing at the trunk. He did it again and again. In the process, the bark scuffed his bare belly and chest, leaving long red and white scratches all over the front of him.

He grunted. He panted hard. He could barely hold back the tears, but he did not cry. He couldn't, not when things at home were the way they were. After trying ten or maybe twenty times he finally managed to get about five feet up the tree. Just two feet more was the lowest branch. He had already used up all his strength. He couldn't bear to look down at what seemed an endless distance stretching below him to the ground. Before he knew it big tears were rolling down his cheeks. Zenta heard his sobbing and came down to the bottom branch.

'Hold on, hold on! One more minute . . .'

Zenta pulled him up the last two feet. Sampei finally stood on the lowermost branch. He couldn't help but laugh through his tears, 'Hmph – hmph – hmph!' It was a weird laugh.

He looked all around. Yes indeed, the tree was high. The view was one he had never seen before. Nevertheless, he could not see all the things he had imagined would be visible – not Mount Fuji, nor a school of whales swimming in the ocean. Still, he didn't think of complaining. He was too busy gazing into the distance – as though he were viewing an entirely new world.

Chapter Fourteen

When Sampei noticed Juzo Akazawa leave with the man from the court, he very nearly shouted a word of greeting. After all, he felt proud to be up in the tree. And he had already forgotten the resentment he felt toward the men when they had barged into his house. Just as he poked his head from the foliage, Zenta pulled him back.

'Zenta, I bet that guy's a cop. Anyhow, I'm glad he didn't take Mom with him.'

'Zenta! Sampei! Come here.' It was Uncle Ukai's voice from inside the house.

The boys quickly slid down the tree. They were on their way to the well to wash their feet when they were told to hurry it up. Mother and Uncle Ukai were in the living room sitting across from each other. The place seemed as topsy-turvy as when Mother was doing the spring cleaning. Things were scattered all over the room. Small white strips of paper had been pasted across the dresser drawers and over the closet doors.

The boys went directly to the living room through the porch without washing off their feet. They sat next to each other, facing their uncle. Sampei in particular looked a fright. He sat stiffly with only his shorts on. Dirt and scratches dappled his face and his body. In ordinary circumstances, Uncle Ukai would have laughed merrily at such a sight, but today his handlebar mustache made him look especially stern as he addressed them:

'I've been talking with your mother about this since yester-day,' he said. 'It seems your family has no more money and nothing that can be turned into money. I've been to the police station and to the factory, but your father will not be back in anything like two or three days. It's possible that the company may take over all your property and land. So your mother will have to go to work and earn money. Since you boys cannot work, you'll have to study hard at school. Do you understand what I'm saying?'

'Well, then, Sampei, you will come with me. In the fall you'll go to school in the country. If you do well in school I'll see you through college. Zenta, you and your mother will stay here for a while, but only until Mother finds a suitable place to stay. Then you will work part-time and go to school there. Okay? Things will not be the same as they have been, so you will have to behave yourselves. Things will be rough for your mother, too. She will have to be brave. You boys will have to mind what people say, so that in a couple of years you can look back and joke about these days.'

Uncle Ukai had to hurry back to his patients, so Mother quickly gathered up some of Sampei's things. There wasn't much to pack because the court had seized most of their property. She bundled his things into a large, square piece of cloth. Then she put his texts and pencils into his knapsack school bag. Sampei looked on like a lost soul.

'Sampei, how about washing your face?' Zenta asked, beckoning him to the well.

'Okay.'

'Well, come on.'

Zenta pumped a bucket full for Sampei. He also brought him the wash basin. He even brought a towel. But the moment Sampei began wiping his face he broke out into a wild wail. It startled Zenta. Mrs Aoyama was so alarmed that she dashed out of the house.

'Sampei, what's wrong?'

He stopped crying that very instant and looked up at her with a smile. She couldn't refrain from asking again, 'What's wrong?'

'It's okay, Mom. I just felt like crying.'

'Well, now,' exclaimed Uncle Ukai, who had also come out to see what was wrong, 'that won't do, wailing like that.'

Mrs Aoyama wrung out the towel and wiped off Sampei's face, chest, and legs. Then she noticed his impish little toes. They were so cute. Seeing them filled her eyes with tears.

Sampei stood there looking up at his mother, his uncle, and his brother. A huge grin spread from ear to ear. Recalling his recent fight with Kintaro he said, 'I wonder if Kin still has that lump I put on his head?'

Chapter Fifteen

Sampei stood in the entranceway with his school bag on his shoulders.

Beside him was his uncle, holding the cloth-wrapped bundle. 'Well, I'll be back tomorrow or the next day,' he said to his sister.

'Be seeing you!' Sampei left just as he did on regular school days.

As they walked through the gate, Mrs Aoyama slipped into her clogs and bolted out the door. Although she had intended to say goodbye from the entranceway, she could not contain herself and hurried to the gate. Sampei had already walked about thirty feet down the road.

'Sampei,' she called gently.

He looked back and smiled. Uncle Ukai turned around and smiled too.

Zenta, who had also decided to come to the gate, stood beside his mother. When Sampei and Uncle Ukai reached the stone bridge by the factory, Sampei – perhaps reminded by his uncle – turned toward the two figures at the gate, took off his school cap and bowed politely. His uncle touched his hand to his hat. They did not look back again.

Zenta watched them fade gradually into the distance. As he turned back through the gate he asked, 'Mom, won't Sampei be coming home any more?'

'Of course he'll come home. He'll be with us during vacations.'

'Gee...'

Zenta didn't go into the house but walked over to the small swing standing by the persimmon tree. He sat in it and pumped gently. It wasn't that he wanted to swing. He wanted to mull things over quietly. But the more he pumped the louder the metal fittings grated. It was a lonely sound. He got off, pulled the empty seat back with both hands and pushed it. The swing went very high. That's what he did when he pushed Sampei.

'There you go!' he would tell his brother. But now he was silent as he pushed it again. When it curved back to him he gave it another push. It made him tired doing it alone. He was just thinking that it was no fun without Sampei when he heard Mother calling.

'Zenta, please get the rest of Sampei's things together. We must have them ready when Uncle Ukai comes back.'

'Okay.'

Zenta took a step toward the house. Then he caught himself. Actually, everying in the yard was Sampei's. The swing was his. So was the persimmon tree. So was half the little rising-sun flag lashed to the tip of the tree. The length of bamboo used the other day to whack the trees and coax out the magic genie – that, too, was Sampei's. And there was the tunnel they had dug to put the frog in, and the wrestling ring they had scratched in the dirt.

Figuring Sampei could make such things at his uncle's, Zenta went to the shed, took out the insect net and fish basket and laid them on the porch. He got Sampei's clogs, sneakers, and his little umbrella from the closet by the front door.

At Sampei's desk he found much more to collect. There were papers from penmanship and composition and arithmetic. They had A's and B's. Zenta read over one of Sampei's compositions:

My Dad

My dad has whiskers. They are scratchy
and hurt. If they brush against me when
we wrestle, I give up then and there.

There was also a small purse in the desk. Zenta opened it and found three coppers. Touched by its poverty, he took out his wallet and emptied it into Sampei's purse. He himself had no more than two coppers and a five-sen piece.

Aside from the purse, Zenta found a few sparklers, a toy blueprint set, and some other stuff. He also spied a squirt gun and took it to the wash basin. He tried to squirt some water but it wasn't much fun without Sampei.

Chapter Sixteen

Sampei and his uncle took a bus for about a dozen miles. They got off and crossed a river. From the bridge they could hear rapids roaring below. The river was quite wide. Beyond the bridge the road led off into a valley. Uncle Ukai's place was another two hundred yards down the road, snuggled against a hill. It was a large house with a thatched roof. Attached to one end was Uncle Ukai's medical office. It had a tile roof. Behind the one-room cottage sitting at the other end of the house stood a white-walled storehouse. Near its entrance was a tall pine with a thick trunk.

As they approached the house Sampei's uncle told him, 'When you get inside, tell your aunt, "I'm sorry to bother you." And be sure you bow. Otherwise, just act as though this were your own house. Make yourself right at home.'

Sampei nodded, 'Sure.'

They had arrived by then. They climbed the three stone steps and stood at the front door.

Uncle Ukai called out, 'I'm back!'

His wife came out to greet them.

'I've brought Sampei to stay with us.'

'Oh you have? Isn't he cute. My, Sampei, are you in school already!'

Sampei doffed his school cap, bowed, and started to carry out his uncle's instructions: 'I'm sorry . . .'

Not another syllable would come out.

'You're what?' his aunt asked.

Before he had a chance to respond, his cousins, Miyoko and Kosuke, came to the front door. Sampei simply stood there for a while, smiling and staring at them. They beamed back at him.

Then all of a sudden he blurted out, 'I'm sorry to . . .' Their faces melted into smiles at the pause, but Sampei was determined

to continue, and he shouted briskly at the top of his lungs, '. . .
bother you.'

They broke into laughter.

'Well, come on in.'

The three children sat on the porch to eat the caramels they
had received. No one said a word. When their eyes met, their
mouths curled into smiles. In the silence, Sampei became aware
of voices coming from the living room. His aunt and uncle were
talking.

'That's simply terrible.' That was his aunt.

'You're right.' That was his uncle's voice.

'And what is Ichiro charged with?'

'They say he forged some documents,' Uncle Ukai said. 'It's a
shame, but it looks like he'll get a year or two for it.'

'My, oh my! Then we'll have to take care of Sampei until his
father's out of jail?'

'You don't get the point. I intend to see him through college.'

'What?' she asked, 'you mean a child like that . . .'

'That's what I mean.'

'They say that if you have a big family,' she continued, 'one
child is sure to be a black sheep. I suppose this means we'll have
to watch over your sister's husband for the rest of our lives.'

'Well, what else can we do?'

'But if we have to look after somebody, I'd just as soon he
hadn't committed a crime.'

'What are you talking about? They haven't yet proved Ichiro
guilty. Even if they had, how can we say anything until we learn
how it all happened?'

After hearing that, Sampei could no longer smile.

Just an hour or so later the Ukais became aware that he was
gone. He wasn't in the house. He wasn't on the grounds. He
wasn't over by the bridge. His uncle and aunt and cousins spread
out and hunted everywhere for him, shouting, 'Sampeeeei!'

Sampei had climbed the tall pine tree in front of the storehouse. It was over a storey high. He sat on a branch, bathed by
the evening sun. He had hoped to get a glimpse of his home, far
in the distance. All he could see were mountains.

Chapter Seventeen

Hoping to get a glimpse of his house wasn't the only reason Sampei had climbed the tall pine. He no longer wanted to stay around after he heard his uncle and aunt talking. He wanted to go and hide. So he sat tight on the branch, even though it was getting dark and he could hear people calling him. He intended to stay there forever. Besides, he had a very interesting view of the sun dipping behind the mountains to the west. It was huge and seemed to be spinning around.

Sampei could hear Uncle Ukai asking a farmer down the road, 'Have you seen a little boy about seven? Just fetched him here from relatives this afternoon and he simply disappeared on us.'

'Oh, is that who he is? I saw 'im a while ago. Up in the pine by your storehouse. See. Looks like a little boy up there. I was sorta uneasy, you know. Dangerous up there . . .'

Dr Ukai was rattled when the farmer pointed to Sampei's hiding place. 'Now, how do you like that? What's he want to climb up there for? Well, really . . .' He hurried back to his yard, stood under the pine, looked up and shouted, 'Hey up there, isn't that you Sampei?'

'Yep, it's me. I'm watchin' the sun. It's really terrific.'

'You're a fine one! Why did you want to climb up there?'

'Okay, I'll come down. I'm on my way,' he said as he got ready to slide down.

'No, Sampei. You stay right where you are. I'm going . . . I'll go get a ladder for you.'

'Aw gee, it's okay. I can slide down. It's okay.'

'No, don't make a move, hear? I'll be right back.'

Thinking how his little sister would feel if anything happened to Sampei, Dr Ukai forgot his dignity – the fame of which had spread for miles around the village – as he ran in confusion to get the ladder.

While his uncle was fetching the ladder, Sampei slid smoothly down the tree. By the time Uncle Ukai reappeared shouldering a long ladder, Sampei was already standing at the foot of the pine. On his uncle's heels were his aunt and his cousins, Miyoko and Kosuke.

Quite impressed by the feat, Aunt Ukai kept saying, 'My, what a fearless little boy! Did you really climb all the way up there?'

Neither of his cousins could utter a word.

Aunt Ukai followed her husband as he took the ladder back. 'What a child!' she said.

'Yes, he has a lot of spirit.'

'Spirit, indeed! He'll certainly get our Kosuke into some very serious trouble before he's through.'

Uncle Ukai said nothing.

His wife pursued the subject. 'You know, dear, I wonder how we can keep such a child in our home.'

The children were sitting on the porch again. Miyoko kept pumping her cousin for information. She was in sixth grade and acted like a big sister. 'Tell us, Sampei, how ever did you climb way up there?'

'Well, just spit on your hands, and you can climb right up.'

After Miyoko had been summoned to the kitchen to help her mother with supper, Sampei started talking.

'Kosuke, how about doing something special?'

'Like what?'

'Something I heard from my big brother. Okay? You take a box about this big,' – he described its size with his hands – 'and write BIRDIE'S LODGE on it. You hang it on the branch of a tree. Then pretty soon some little bird comes and stays in it. How about it?'

That was enough to get Kosuke interested.

'No kidding?'

'No kidding.'

'Well,' Kosuke proposed, 'let's try it tomorrow.'

'Okay, let's do it.'

They agreed to make birdhouses in the morning.

Chapter Eighteen

Kosuke and Sampei were busy from the moment they got up. They laid out a saw, a hammer and nails, and a broken fruit box on the front porch. They sawed and hammered so intently that their heads almost touched the floorboards.

Of course they ignored everything else, including Miyoko. Not even her 'What're you making?' got an answer. She asked again, this time shaking her brother's shoulder. 'Kosuke, what are you making?'

Finally he looked up. 'A box.'

'What're you going to do with it?'

'Make a house,' he said.

'A house?'

After that he refused to say a word, despite her many questions. The boys were absolutely immersed in their project. Once Miyoko realized that they were trying to make boxes, however, she could not bear to look on and see them bungle the job. Sampei's effort in particular didn't look as though it ever would become a box. She reached out her hand, 'Sampei, lemme see it.'

She took the saw, trimmed the edges of the slats straight across and made sure they were of equal length. Then she nailed them together, ending up – more or less – with something that looked like a box. Well, it was a kind of pyramid-shaped 'box', resembling a can of corned beef. She was proud of her handiwork nevertheless.

'How's this?' she asked.

'Great!' Sampei was completely satisfied with it. He held it at arm's length and inspected it. He pictured a little bird lying down inside, sleeping with its head on a small pillow, its legs stretched out comfortably.

'Swell! Terrific, it's just terrific!' As far as he was concerned this was a splendid birdhouse. He was impatient to get it labelled BIRDIE'S LODGE.

Kosuke's box was finished too. It had been put together, at any rate, though when Miyoko saw it she blurted out, 'You mean that's a box?'

'Sure it's a box,' Kosuke said. He wasn't exactly happy with the results, for no one could possibly tell whether it was a triangle or a square. It was, in fact, nearly shapeless. One end stuck out some five-eighths of an inch beyond the joint. The other was half an inch short of forming a joint. Kosuke had not nailed together one end of his 'box'.

'Well, maybe it is a box,' admitted Miyoko, staring at it first from the front and then from the rear.

'It's a box,' Kosuke said. He was upset by her attitude. But he calmed down when he thought of it as a birdhouse hanging from a tree.

'Sis, how about writing on it for me?'

'Write what?' Miyoko asked.

'What was it anyhow? BIRD HOUSE? No ... or was it BIRDIE HOUSE?'

'Neither one,' said Sampei. 'It was BIRDIE'S LODGE.'

'Oh, BIRDIE INN?' asked Miyoko.

'No. It was BIRDIE'S LODGE,' Kosuke said, pouting.

'Well, okay ...' Miyoko said. She then fetched the India ink and a brush and lettered the boxes for them. Of course she printed in large block letters so that little birds could read it with no trouble. And she wrote on either side so that no bird would miss the message.

When she finished, the boys rummaged around for some lengths of cord to tie their house to a limb. With the cord safely in their pockets, they were ready to leave.

'They're birdhouses, aren't they? You're going to hang them in the woods, right?' Miyoko asked.

'Naw, we're not either,' Kosuke protested. The boys firmly rebuffed her when she said she would tag along.

'Beat it!' they said, and dashed off toward the woods.

Despite the rebuff, Miyoko followed them. About thirty minutes later she came screaming into the house, 'Mother, a terrible thing has happened. Kosuke and Sampei've climbed to the top of the oak.'

Chapter Nineteen

As punishment for climbing the oak to hang their birdhouses, the boys were sternly forbidden to enter the woods again. And the next day they were allowed to go to the river on condition that they would not go into the water. They could only look down at the stream from the top of the levee.

Kosuke and Sampei were standing on the levee, as they had promised, watching the activity in the river. They saw about a dozen sun-tanned boys of various ages splashing around and yelling to one another. A couple of the boys called out to Kosuke.

'Hi, Kosuke. Come on down.'

'Why aren't you swimming?'

Kosuke went to the water's edge and squatted down. Sampei trailed along and squatted beside him. But the boys talked only to Kosuke, so Sampei felt left out. He was sick of saying nothing and merely watching those who swam so energetically in the river. Then he overheard two grown-ups talking on the top of the levee.

'You saw it in the paper, didn't you? About Ichiro Aoyama?'

'Hmmm. And that's his kid, is it?'

After hearing that, he couldn't sit still for another moment. He looked all around and saw, about thirty feet off, a place where the village women did their laundry. A large, half-submerged tub caught his eye. It certainly looked interesting. Sampei walked over to it. Now that was fascinating – the tub fluttered cheerfully in the water every time a wave lapped against its side. He stepped into it. It bobbed just like a ship. At that moment he was doubly or triply glad that he had found the tub to play in. He told himself that he would have a tremendous time with it.

First he got out and found a bamboo pole four or five feet long. Then he used the pole to push the tub away from the riverbank. It was floating free. Now the tub was his ship. He pushed it along the edge of the bank, utterly enjoying himself as he sang, 'Ruba-dubdub, my ship is a tub.'

He wanted everyone to know he was having a good time. No one said a word. No one was even watching. What was the use of all his work? So he boarded the tub and began singing, 'Ruba-dubdub, my big ship the tub.' Nobody paid any attention to him.

By then his ship was about sixty feet from the boys who were swimming. Sampei was still close enough to the riverbank to step onto dry land if he wanted to get out of the tub. Now, he figured, was the time to make a bold move. He had made up his mind. He pushed against the bank with his pole, sending his ship into midstream. The current was swift, and in a twinkling it sent the tub whirling and racing downstream, gathering speed by the minute. Crying out in alarm was out of the question – it would sully his manly honor – so Sampei continued singing as though nothing had happened: 'Rubadubdub, a boy in a tub. Rubadub-dub, my big ship the tub.'

He had been swept another fifty or sixty feet downstream. He could hear the roar of rapids ahead. In another moment he found himself running them. The swift flow tossed his tub about. Sampei clung to the sides of the tub with both hands.

'Gosh – mountains of waves!'

His face turned pale, but he never thought of crying out for help. Neither did he have the presence of mind to enjoy the scenery. To an onlooker, however, he appeared to be enjoying himself immensely as he bobbed through the rapids.

The boys who had been swimming were in an uproar. Shouting, they ran along the bank, chasing the tub. In another quarter mile or so the stream emptied into a large river where flatboats plied. But before that, Sampei would have to negotiate some deep places with whirlpools and pass over cascades.

Uncle Ukai was returning on horseback from house calls when he heard the commotion the boys were stirring up. He shouted from the top of the levee, 'What's going on down there? What's wrong?'

The moment he learned about Sampei, he spurred his horse and flew along the levee road as though it were a race track. The bank was dotted with bamboo thickets which prevented a clear view. At every break in the bamboo, Uncle Ukai stopped his horse and scanned the river. Though he had travelled several hundred yards downstream, he found no trace of Sampei.

Chapter Twenty

Dr Ukai raced along the bank looking for Sampei. At each
opening in the bamboo he searched the river for the tub. At the
fifth opening it occurred to him that Sampei couldn't possibly
have been carried off such a distance.

He saw a laundering spot at the water's edge. A path led to it
from the levee road. Uncle Ukai followed the road to the stream
and urged his horse into the water. Once in the middle of the
river, he looked upstream and downstream for a trace of his
nephew.

'He must still be upstream from here,' he said to himself. He
turned his horse into the flow and splashed through the water. He
wanted the horse to hurry, but the water was above its shanks.
All the while, Uncle Ukai carefully scoured the stream looking
for Sampei. Had the tub sunk? Had Sampei been swept under
water?

A hundred or so yards upstream he came to a sharp bend
where the water formed a very deep pool. Dr Ukai rode onto the
bank. He would have to take a good look into the depths of the
pool. Just then he thought he heard somebody calling him. He
looked around. There he was. There was Sampei sitting in his
tub, just a short distance ahead in a pocket formed by a boulder
that jutted into the stream.

'Sampei!' he shouted in an unexpectedly loud voice.

'I got carried away.'

Uncle Ukai responded automatically, 'It's okay. It's okay.'

'Gosh, was that scary! That water's really fast.'

Sampei's uncle had meanwhile taken the rope from behind his
saddle and thrown the loose end to Sampei. 'Come on now, get
hold of it. Okay, got a good grip? It'd be terrible if you got
dunked now.'

Then he pulled the tub, Sampei and all, back to where his

horse had first entered the stream. He dismounted, secured the rope, and lifted his nephew out of the tub.

'My, oh my! Well, you're safe now. Sampei, you really gave me a scare.'

'Were you worried about me?'

'You bet I was. I felt pretty sure you had already drowned.'

'Oh, I wouldn't drown. This stream is lots smaller than the ocean.'

'Don't be silly, boy. Small or not, a couple of kids like you drown in this very stream every summer.'

Uncle Ukai pulled the tub out of the water, put Sampei on the saddle, mounted his horse, and urged it up the levee.

'Everyone is worried about you, so we'll gallop back. Giddyap!' he said, spurring the horse on.

Sampei enjoyed himself immensely. He couldn't help smiling. Still, he was somewhat anxious about his ship.

'What about the tub?'

'It'll be all right. We'll have somebody pick it up later.'

When they neared the village, a number of boys came running toward them, huffing and puffing, their faces strained. At the sight of Sampei riding with his uncle, they spontaneously cheered, 'Hurrah!' Though the horse soon left them behind, they continued running after it, shouting all the way. By the time the boys reached the swimming hole, their number had swelled to twenty.

A dozen or so adults had gathered on the bank and on the levee. They went up to offer Dr Ukai their sympathy,.

'You surely had a scare, sir!'

'Thank God the boy's safe!'

Embarrassed by the attention, Sampei asked his uncle to let him down from the saddle. He quickly grabbed Kosuke's hand and headed for home. The village boys continued to surround him and pepper him with questions.

'Wasn't it scary?'

'Naw,' Sampei answered. 'It was fun.'

Chapter Twenty-One

Sampei became the idol of the village boys after his tub ride down the river. A number of them came to the gate calling, 'Sampeeei! Come on out and play.'

After the tub incident, however, Sampei was not allowed to play with them. He was even forbidden to play with Kosuke. That left Miyoko, who had been put in charge of him.

'Sampei, how about origami? I'll fold a crane for you.'

It wasn't that Sampei disliked Miyoko. Girls' games just bored him to death.

'Sampei, how about playing store? I'll be the candy store manager. You come to buy some candy.'

He soon got sick of games like that, too.

So they went to the woods to collect bugs and flowers. Bell-flowers and maiden-flowers were in bloom. Katydids were chirping in the grass. Even while he was picking flowers and chasing insects, Sampei heard from far and near the lively voices of the village boys.

'You'd rather be playing with them, wouldn't you?' Miyoko asked.

'Naw,' he replied, shaking his head.

Actually, Sampei was not having much fun. That is, he didn't enjoy himself until – as he chased after a katydid – he found that the tall grass completely concealed him.

Miyoko missed him and became anxious. Looking around she called, 'Sampei! Sampei! Where are you?'

That was more like fun to hear her calling him. Whenever he had the chance, he hid himself in the grass. Only after Miyoko said, 'You meany. All right for you, I'm not looking any-more!' did Sampei emerge from his hiding place, laughing hysterically.

When that was no longer any fun, he started hiding in trees. He

climbed noiselessly, keeping out of her line of vision. When he
reached the leaves, he called, 'Miyokoooo . . .'

'Where are you Sampei? Come on, you're teasing me again.'

When she caught sight of the leaves moving, she acted as
though she was terribly put out.

'Sampei, what am I going to do with you? Mother'll scold me,
so please come on down.' She pretended she was on the verge of
tears.

After two or three times her act lost its effect. Then, whenever
she spied Sampei climbing a tree, she went straight over and
started shaking it.

'Watch it, watch it,' she said 'or you'll fall, you'll fall.'

They emerged from the woods near a mountain pond. On one
side of the valley was a high bank. The other three sides were
hemmed in by steep slopes crammed with tall trees mirrored on
the deep, vivid green of the pond's surface. It was such a tremendous sight that it overwhelmed even Sampei.

'How about it, Sampei? I bet you don't have a pond like this
where you live, do you?'

'Nope,' he said. He had no choice but to agree.

'Isn't it scary though?'

It really was a scary pond. The water's edge was only twelve or
fifteen feet from where they stood. A turtle floated on the surface, his legs stretched out, his head raised. He looked the
picture of ease.

'Once I went swimming here,' Miyoko continued. 'I couldn't
make it to the other side but I got halfway. Can you swim,
Sampei? I bet you can't.'

Sampei didn't answer. What could he say?

'You weren't afraid of the river but you're afraid of this pond.
Hahahaha!'

Chapter Twenty-Two

Sampei couldn't take that lying down. 'I could make it,' he said soberly.

'You think you can do better than me? Well, show me you can swim.'

'I can swim.'

'I don't believe you.'

'I can too.'

'Even if the pond's scary? Besides, it's got snakes in it. Anyhow, Sampei,' Miyoko said as she pointed to the floating turtle, 'you know about guardian spirits, don't you? A huge turtle is the guardian of the pond. It's supposed to be a dozen or more times as big as this one. And there's a *kappa* besides. Once when Mr Yokotani came by to cut some grass he saw the *kappa* playing on the back of the guardian turtle. You know about *kappas*, Sampei?'

'Nope.'

'You mean to say you've never heard of a *kappa*? All the boys around here know about them. A *kappa* has a plate on top of his head filled with water. As long as he has water in it a *kappa* is supposed to be very strong. He can drag kids and even grown-ups into the water. Isn't that scary?'

'Nope.'

'You're not scared? If the *kappa* hears you he's sure to come out and drag you into the pond.'

'Let 'im.'

'You don't get it, Sampei. He really comes and drags kids into the pond. Hairs hang down from his head. His hands and feet have long claws. He floats up to the surface of the water and pops out. It's scary, really scary. C'mon, let's get going. It's too scary for me.'

Sampei wouldn't budge. Though she tugged at his arm, he held his ground. 'I'm not going,' he said in his most serious tone. 'I'm staying to see the *kappa*.'

'Oh, you're not going to pull that again!' Miyoko was quite upset. 'Why do you keep saying things like that?'

'Because.'

'What kind of answer is that? You just don't know anything about it, Sampei. What a lot of trouble you cause us! Mom says you're an impossible child. You really do take chances, you know. She says we're going to send you back home if you keep doing scary things like climbing high trees and floating down the river. You hear? Now be a good boy.'

'I'm not going. I'm staying here. You go back by yourself.'

'What'll you do here?'

Sampei refused to talk any more. For a while Miyoko stood silently, gazing at the pond. 'Well,' she finally said, 'I'm going home and tell Mom and Dad. You stay put.' With that she ran off toward home, down the hill and into the woods, looking over her shoulder again and again.

Sampei stared solemnly into the pond. He figured that the *kappa*'s platter-like head with hair dangling from it would pop out of the water any second. But he wasn't sitting there just because he wanted to wait for the *kappa*. The real reason he stayed behind was that he didn't want to go back to his uncle's. If only he could walk that far, he wanted to go home to Mother and Zenta. He also wanted to know what was happening to his dad, but that was one thing he couldn't bring himself to ask anyone about.

Miyoko ran all the way home. She panted as she explained to her mother, 'He wouldn't move . . . he just kept saying . . . he'd wait to see the *kappa* . . . oh, Mom . . . come and see . . . come on, please!'

Mrs Ukai's face clouded. 'He's getting worse and worse. There's a limit to what I can bear. We'll wait for Daddy to come home. He'll know what to tell Sampei. In the meantime, the boy may come back on his own.'

'But Mom, what if the *kappa* gets him?'

'Don't be silly.'

They put Sampei out of their thoughts. One hour passed. Two hours. Still he did not return. Just before sunset, Miyoko and Kosuke went to the pond to bring him back.

Sampei wasn't there!

The news caused a stir throughout the village. All the men assembled and formed searching parties. They dragged the pond. They combed the woods and hunted through the whole valley.

Chapter Twenty-Three

Sampei had gone to stay with his uncle. Father was still at the police station. Mother had left earlier for town. It was lonely and eerie, but Zenta had no choice. He had to watch the house.

A loquat tree stood next to the porch. As he moped around the yard, Zenta spied two tree frogs at the fork in its trunk. There was a big one and a small one. Lined up like good friends, they seemed plastered to the tree. They didn't blink their eyes. They didn't move. Could they be alive?

When he looked more closely, Zenta noticed a gentle movement under their chins. Concluding that the frogs were indeed alive, it occurred to him that the pair seemed like brothers. The big one was Zenta, the little one was Sampei.

'These fellows like to sleep with their eyes wide open,' Zenta mumbled to himself. He had been watching the house for a long time, so he felt like talking to somebody.

'Hey you, wake up. Wake up and talk to your brother.'

He banged on the tree. Neither frog stirred. Then he remembered that if you stroked frogs gently under the chin, they might let out a croak.

'That's it.'

Zenta went in and got a small pair of tongs. He wrapped cotton around the ends, with which he gingerly touched the smaller frog's throat. He moved the cotton tips back and forth, trying to tickle the little fellow.

'Croak for me. Come on, croak.'

He said it softly. Rather than cooperate, the frog began crawling leisurely away, as though he intended to climb to the top of the tree.

'Idiot. If you go any higher the sparrows'll find you and gobble you up.'

There were indeed some sparrows chirping on the porch roof.

Not in the least afraid of them, the little frog kept on climbing higher and higher. The big one stretched out his front legs, making himself more comfortable, and let out a croak.

'Hey, he croaked,' Zenta blurted out.

Zenta figured the big one was calling to his brother, so he leaned toward the little one and said, 'Say, your big brother's calling you.'

The little frog continued climbing.

'You're really just like him – you don't listen to anybody.' Zenta was thinking of Sampei.

He watched the frog turn into a small green dot on the top branch, some dozen feet above the ground. He looked like a piece of grass stuck on the side of the tree. Then, just as Zenta had feared, the flutter of wings in the treetop! At almost the same moment, something fell past Zenta, something that looked like a piece of dew, something green that whizzed by his face.

'Dog-gone! Just like I said.'

The smaller frog ended up squatting on the ground under the tree, his forelegs stretched out in front of him. He started hopping around as though he suddenly remembered he could jump. Zenta, who wanted to put him back on the tree next to his big brother, used both hands trying to get hold of him. But the little fellow, leaping and dancing around, managed to escape.

'Aw, to heck with it. A snake'll get you sooner or later. And after all the trouble I went to, trying to put you back.'

It began raining, so Zenta went inside. It seemed an hour before the rain stopped and the sun came out. A faint rainbow spanned the sky.

Zenta returned to the tree and found the two frogs lined up again like good buddies. He picked up a large loquat leaf that had fallen to the ground and made a roof by laying it in the crotch above them. He felt sorry for them.

'Now you've got a roof. That'll be your house. Don't go away now,' he told them.

Clinging to the tree under their roof, and apparently asleep, neither frog moved.

Chapter Twenty-Four

Zenta was watching the house again. Mother had left early for town on business concerning Father and the trouble at the factory. Zenta, having nothing to do, rambled around the house and yard.

A dragonfly had landed on the swing rope. Under the persimmon he saw five or six ants dragging a small moth. The tree frogs no longer clung to the loquat tree, though the leaf that had served as their roof was still there.

As he dangled his legs from the porch Zenta thought, 'If only Sampei was here. We'd be playing hide-and-seek by now.'

He'd have to play alone.

'Are you ready?' he called out.

'Not yet,' he answered in a far-off voice – or rather, in one squeezed to give it distance.

'Ready?'

'Ready!'

'Here I come, ready or not.'

Zenta's heart felt a bit lighter now. He could even laugh again.

'I wonder where he is. In the bathroom? By the persimmon tree out back? Maybe in the shed?'

He went to the shed first.

'Gotcha! You're in there,' he shouted, standing outside the door. He could almost hear Sampei's peculiar clucking kind of chuckle.

'Gotcha! Come on out.' He opened the door. Not there.

'Well, he must be in the bathroom.' Zenta went to the bathroom and threw the door open. 'Aha! There you are.'

Nobody was there.

'Well, then, he has to be out back by the persimmon tree. He's up in the tree for sure.' Zenta ran to the back yard.

'Hey, I found ya!' he called before he was anywhere near the tree. He figured it was time to find Sampei.

Now it was his turn. Zenta decided to hide in the house.

'Not yeeet,' he yelled as he dashed here and there looking for a good place to hide. He opened the closet door. No good. He looked under the desk. In the alcove. In the cabinet. Not one good hiding place among them. He stood in the back room trying to make up his mind. In front of him he saw one of Father's kimonos hanging on a nail.

'That's it!' He hid behind the kimono.

No sooner had he concealed himself than he somehow felt the game a bit silly. He couldn't keep from laughing, no matter how hard he tried. Yet when he pricked up his ears he thought he heard Sampei calling, 'Ready?'

'Ready,' Zenta answered.

How long was it? He waited and waited. Sampei never came. Zenta closed his eyes, but all he saw was Sampei. In his mind's eye Zenta watched his little brother trudging up a far-off hill, his school bag on his shoulders.

'Okay, I'm ready.'

However often he cried *Ready*! Sampei never came. Zenta kept seeing his little brother march over the hill and get smaller and smaller.

He was about to roar 'Sampei!' when something touched him through Father's kimono. Startled, Zenta opened his eyes. He peeked out. Something was there, something pitch black.

Once in a book of fairy tales he had seen a picture of a witch with eyes that glared out of the black cloth that enveloped her. He trembled.

'It must have been my imagination,' Zenta thought. 'I'm not going to find anything when I pop out of here.' Mustering some courage, he jumped out and dashed across the room shouting, 'Heeeeeey!'

Indeed, no witch was there. It was broad daylight.

Chapter Twenty-Five

The man was wearing a pair of high rubber boots. He had the ends of his dirty summer kimono tucked up and was carrying piggy-back a child of two or three. Or rather, the child had been strapped on his back with a piece of cloth and was wailing loudly, 'Mommy . . . Mommy . . . !'

Between every two or three cries the child whimpered pitifully. The man didn't let the screaming and weeping bother him in the least. He walked quickly, taking long strides. The child continued screaming, 'Mommy . . . Mommy . . . Mommy . . . !'

The cry was enough to make the stones weep.

Though the child had wailed dozens of times, the man was not one bit flustered. But Zenta could not ignore it. He had encountered the man on the way back from an errand to the lawyer's. It was on the edge of town and the man had appeared from one side street and was disappearing into another.

In a flash Zenta thought, 'He's a kidnapper. He's kidnapping that baby.'

Zenta was sure the child's mother would be pursuing the man. He stopped and looked for her. He couldn't see her anywhere. Passers-by were indifferent. Zenta thought, 'If only a policeman would come along now!'

Meanwhile, the kidnapper wheeled speedily on.

Zenta felt so impatient that he stood there stomping his feet. But he could do no more than follow the man. Sooner or later he was sure that somebody would realize the man was a kidnapper. Or that a policeman would come along. Or that even the child's mother would be in breathless pursuit. These thoughts ran through Zenta's mind as he followed the kidnapper, keeping about sixty feet behind him.

The child never stopped shrieking, 'Mommy . . . Mommy . . . . ! Every time the child cried out Zenta felt as though he himself were screaming. He felt as though the last thin thread connecting him to his mother was about to snap. He was clinging to it and crying out as loud as he could.

The kidnapper turned a corner in the path and disappeared. When Zenta reached the corner he could no longer see him. Nor could he hear the child screaming. Zenta stood on the corner for a while, looking all around and straining his ears. Finally he turned back toward home.

'The kidnapper's house must be over there somewhere.' He walked along, thinking about what he had seen. He could not get the child's plaintive wail out of his head. When he got home he wanted to ask his mother about it, but for some reason he couldn't bring the subject up.

That night he dreamed about his experience.

'Zenta, Zenta!' Mother's voice awakened him.

'What's wrong, honey? You've been crying in your sleep for some time.'

'Me crying?'

'Yes, you were crying. I thought you were awake.'

'Gosh, I had a nightmare.'

'What kind of nightmare?'

'Say, Mom . . .'

Zenta didn't feel like telling Mother he had dreamed that Sampei was kidnapped.

'Mom, are there really such things as kidnappers?'

'There's no such thing.'

'No kidding?'

He looked drowsy, as though he were still asleep. Then he sat bolt upright and asked, 'Mom, didn't Sampei come back?'

Mother looked surprised at first. Then she became cross with him. 'What are you talking about? Sampei come back in the middle of the night?'

'I just had the feeling he had come home.'

Chapter Twenty-Six

Zenta found some woman's sandals and a pair of small shoes in the entranceway when he returned from an errand.

'Hey, they look like Sampei's shoes.'

A smile slipped out and climbed over his cheek. He nevertheless managed to announce in a sober tone, 'I'm back!' He went inside and found his mother talking to Aunt Ukai in the living room. He bowed and sat down beside them.

He wanted ever so much to ask where Sampei was, but somehow couldn't get the words out. He got up and started looking. Sampei wasn't in the dining room, or in the kitchen, or in the back room.

But that was certainly his cap and his schoolbag on the hat-rack by the entrance. There was no need to ask. Sampei was home.

Zenta went outside to look for him. There, under the persimmon tree, he found his mother's big clogs. Sampei had climbed the tree. Zenta climbed up and met him in the branches. They smiled at each other but neither uttered a word.

Though Sampei had been gone only a week, they felt somewhat shy. Zenta found it hard to say Sampei's name. Sampei found it hard to say Zenta's. Even if he wanted to, Zenta could not possibly have told Sampei how he had cried in his sleep when he dreamed that his brother was kidnapped. Sampei felt exactly the same way. Still, they couldn't go on just smiling at each other forever.

Sampei started down. In only five or six days he had become an expert and slid down skillfully. He showed Zenta how well he could slide. His big brother slid down no less expertly. When Zenta reached the ground Sampei started climbing back up. He was good at that now, too. After several climbing contests, the brothers found themselves standing under the tree.

Zenta boldly yelled, 'Hey Sampei!'

'What?'

With that they grappled and started a pushing contest. They knew of no other way to deal with their joy and shyness.

'Gee,' Zenta said, 'you sure are weak.'

'What do you mean?' Sampei's face reddened as he poured every ounce of strength into his arms and legs.

'That's more like it,' Zenta praised him. 'That's better.'

'I'm plenty strong,' Sampei said, straining wildly and grunting loudly. He had long since pushed Zenta out of the wrestling circle.

'You are pretty strong,' Zenta admitted.

Still Sampei kept on pushing.

'I give in, I give in,' Zenta cried.

But Sampei refused to let up.

'Come on, I said you won.'

By then Sampei had pushed Zenta into the cypress tree all the way back by the hedge.

'I surrender, I surrender. Cut it out and I'll give you my pencil.'

With that Sampei finally stopped pushing. But they were able to talk freely only after Sampei actually had Zenta's pencil in his hand.

Zenta started the conversation. 'Sampei, what happened? Aren't you going back to the Ukais'?'

'Nope. Uncle Ukai says I'm too naughty. So he'll take you instead.'

'Take me?'

'Right.'

'No thanks.'

'What do you mean, no thanks? It's lots of fun there. They've got a big pond. It's got a turtle in it. They say he's the guardian spirit of the pond. A real whopper. And a *kappa* plays on his back. Lots 'a fun.'

'Crap!'

Chapter Twenty-Seven

Sampei suddenly seemed to remember something. 'Oh, I almost forgot.' He went to the front door and opened the closet.

'What're you looking for?' Zenta asked, trailing along behind him.

'Nothin'.'

After peeking into the closet, Sampei went around the porch to the back door.

'What's up? Looking for your shoes?'

'Nope,' Sampei said, shaking his head. Nevertheless, it did seem that he was searching for something.

'Come on, tell me what you're hunting for. I'll help you look.'

Sampei didn't answer.

After looking around by the back door, he returned in silence to the persimmon tree and sat down on the tin can. He didn't say a word.

After a while, Zenta asked gently, 'You're looking for your sneakers, aren't you?'

'Nope,' Sampei answered, shaking his head again.

'Well, what is it?' Zenta leaned forward in anticipation.

'Zenta . . .'

'Yeah?'

But Sampei didn't say anything.

'Come on. What is it? Tell me what you're looking for.'

Sampei looked squarely into Zenta's puzzled eyes and asked softly, 'What's happened to Daddy?'

Sampei had been looking to see whether he could find the clogs his dad had been wearing when he went off to the police station. Nobody had told him a word of news about the topic he was most interested in – Father. Sampei couldn't bring himself to ask questions about him. Now, for the first time, he was able to ask.

Zenta didn't answer. He hung his head and looked at the

ground. After a while he started biting his lip. Tears welled up in his eyes.

Seeing Zenta's reaction, Sampei casually got up from the oil can and walked toward the shed as though he were still looking for something. As he approached the shed he picked up a stick. Then he squatted down and began scratching in the dirt. His breathing trembled under the sobs. Tears began to spill down his cheeks.

He had no idea what he was drawing, but he kept at it. He made a big circle. He put in eyes and a nose. He attached ears to both sides and even added a long, stiff mustache under the nose.

As he was scratching out his picture, he wiped the tears that rolled down his cheeks with the back of the hand that held the stick. When he finished putting in the mustache, he dropped the stick. He had choked up with tears and needed both hands to cover his face.

After a while Zenta came up, his face as streaked with tears as Sampei's. By then Sampei had managed to stop crying. He was staring at the picture he had just scratched into the dirt. He pointed to the huge face and said with great pride. 'Say, Zenta, what'd you do if a spook like this showed up?'

'No spook like that's gonna come around.'

'But what if he did? What'd you do?'

'He won't.'

'Okay, so he won't. But I'm saying, what if he did?'

'No spook like that'll show up. So there's no use thinking about if he did.'

'Well . . . anyhow, I wouldn't be scared if one like this showed up.'

'Of course you wouldn't,' Zenta answered.

'Well, how about if one like this turned up?'

Sampei quickly scratched two horns on top of the mammoth face and added two rows of jagged teeth.

'He doesn't scare me either,' Zenta said.

'Then how about this one?'

Sampei added another pair of horns.

Chapter Twenty-Eight

Aunt Ukai finally left after her long talk. She was in a good mood.

'Goodbye, Sampei. Be a good boy.'

After she was gone, Mrs Aoyama called the boys into the dining room. She asked Sampei, 'Just what did you do at your uncle's?'

'Nothing,' Sampei answered.

'You climbed way up a high tree, didn't you?'

'Yep, but I got down all by myself.'

'You got in a tub and were swept down the river, weren't you?'

'But that stream was real fast. I never figured on being swept away. It caught me and took me off. Never saw a river like that.'

'Well, that's not so bad. But why,' Mother continued, 'did you hide from everybody at the pond? Your aunt said you caused a tremendous commotion. Isn't that true? She says the whole village was out hunting for you. And all the while you were asleep in the closet.'

'Yep.'

'Why did you do such naughty things?'

Sampei pouted. 'But I didn't do anything,' he protested. 'I wanted to see the *kappa* ride on the turtle's back. I waited at the edge of the pond. But he never came out. So I went back to the house. That's all.'

'Then why did you hide in the closet?'

''Cause ... well, Auntie was saying things about me. And besides, I was sleepy.'

From Sampei's viewpoint, there were reasons for everything he did. She couldn't blame him for what had happened.

Mother only said, 'Well, I wonder...' She was mulling over the problem in her mind.

Then Zenta asked, 'But Mom, what'll we do now?'

'The Ukais say they won't keep Sampei any more because he

might get hurt,' she said. 'But they think you'd be all right, Zenta. Aunt Ukai says she'll be glad to take you home any time. What do you want to do, Zenta? I've been running around so much these days . . . I asked your aunt to wait awhile till we decide.'

'Oh . . .?' Zenta's face clouded.

He was quite prepared to adjust. After all, his family was in a jam. But at the last minute he could not very well change all the plans for the future which he had outlined in his mind. He had been looking forward to the end of August when he and his mother were to move to the clinic where she would work as receptionist. Their room would be very small. But it was plenty big enough for the two of them to sleep in.

A year ago when Zenta had appendicitis he had stayed at the clinic. He knew the set-up. There was a black-and-white cat called Bloom who had produced six cute kittens. All along the hallway hung bird cages full of paddy birds, linnets, and canaries. And there was Goro, the old dog who sprawled out by the entranceway.

Aside from his homework, all Zenta had to do was walk Goro in the morning after he got up, feed the birds, and go to school. The Director was a kind man and the nurses were all pretty.

But now Zenta might have to go to the Ukai's instead. His dreams melted away in a flash. What experiences awaited him in the country?

Suddenly his brother's voice interrupted his thoughts.

'Mom, how about if nobody goes anywhere?' Sampei suggested, beaming as though he had made a great discovery. 'We'll just stay here and wait for Daddy to come home.'

She smiled sadly. 'If only we could . . .'

'We can. Me and Zenta, we'll do everything – cooking and washing and heating the bath water. Then we can go earn money. Say Zenta, how about it? How about starting tomorrow? If you show me, I can even cook the rice. Okay, Mommy . . .?'

The idea entranced Sampei.

Chapter Twenty-Nine

Mrs Aoyama had just crawled into bed when she heard somebody rustling around the room. She called out, wondering whether it was Zenta or Sampei, 'Who's up?'

'It's me.'

'Sampei?'

'Yep.'

'What is it?'

'Mom, what time is it?'

'It's ten. I just got to bed.'

'You did?'

Sampei was already back in bed when he asked, 'Mommy, it's still a long way to morning, right?'

'You bet.'

Sampei planned to make breakfast in the morning. He got up in another hour or two and pussy-footed about the house.

'What's wrong, Sampei?'

'What time is it?'

'Oh my, is it eleven by now? Maybe it's midnight.'

Sampei went back to bed, but he didn't sleep very soundly.

At about four o'clock in the morning he moved close to Zenta, sleeping like a rock next to him, and called softly into his ear, 'Zenta, let's get up.'

Zenta couldn't get his eyes open.

Sampei called again, 'It's morning already.'

'Whaaat?'

'Aren't you going to make breakfast?'

'What for?' Zenta had forgotten what they talked about last night.

'What d'ya mean, what for? Didn't we promise to take care of the cooking, starting today?'

'The cooking? Why'd we wanna do that?'

'Didn't you say you would yesterday?'

Zenta finally sat up. Mother was still sound asleep. After all, it was not yet dawn. They crawled out of the mosquito net and left the room quietly.

In the kitchen the boys found a pot on the range and the soup kettle on the charcoal stove. They lifted the lid and discovered the pot already had rice in it. Mother had filled the kettle with water. She had even stuffed some kindling into the range. A pile of firewood was stacked nearby. On top of the wood were some matches.

Nothing to it!

'Zenta, all you have to do is light it.'

'Right.'

'Come on, hurry and light it.'

They squatted down and squeezed together in front of the range. Zenta lit a match to the kindling. When it flared up, he took four sticks of firewood and crammed them into the opening. Zenta blew into the opening, his lips puckered, his cheeks puffed out. The smoke made his eyes water. Sampei put his face next to Zenta's and began blowing, too. But smoke only billowed out and their efforts were wasted.

'Hurry and get the fan,' Zenta ordered.

Sampei rushed off to the dining room. Some smoke had already rolled there ahead of him. Once they began to fan, the fire started burning properly, full of life. They were delighted when the wood caught.

'Hey, that was something, eh Zenta?'

It was a warm summer morning, yet Sampei stretched out his hands toward the fire. As he was warming himself, some steam popped against the cover. Startled, the boys stood up. 'What's that, Zenta?'

'It's okay. We just have to take off the top,' Zenta said as he removed it. The pot boiled over nevertheless. Then they tried fanning away the bubbles. When the water stopped foaming they put the lid back on. Whenever it started boiling up again they removed the cover and fanned.

By now the smell told them that the rice was burnt. Clearly they had botched the job. But it was too late to do anything about it. Sampei scampered off to tell Mother.

'Mommy, come quick. The rice is all burned.'

Chapter Thirty

'Don't worry about it,' Mother said. 'If the two of you will get out of my way, I'll make breakfast.'

Neither boy budged an inch.

'Aw, c'mon, Mom. You get out of our way and we'll cook up a good breakfast for you,' Sampei said, pushing her back toward the dining room.

'That's right, Mom. The rest is a cinch,' Zenta added as he helped his brother push her out of the kitchen. 'All we have to do now is the soup.'

'Stop it! Now stop it, I say!'

They only pushed harder.

'We can do it.'

'Yep, we can do it.'

They shoved her with all their might beyond the dining room all the way to the front door.

'Now that's enough, boys. This isn't funny any more.'

They ran back to the kitchen as she was talking and closed the door behind them. They held it so she couldn't open it. She had no choice but to surrender.

'All right, then, you make breakfast. Mother has other work to do. But if you have any problems, come and ask me. All right?'

'Fine,' they answered heartily.

They started cooking again.

'Say, Zenta, what is it you said we make now?'

'Soup.'

'How do we make it?'

'Well, we . . . gee, how do you make it? Oh yeah, that's right. First we light the charcoal stove.'

'How?'

'Well, ah . . . in winter there's always some coals in the hibachi, but . . .'

'Lemme go ask.'

Sampei scampered off to ask Mother.

'Mom, we want to light the charcoal stove. How do we do it? Zenta's all mixed up about it.'

'My, oh my, oh my!' she said, unable to keep from chuckling. 'You probably have some fire in the range. Use the tongs to transfer an ember to the stove and put some charcoal on top of it.'

'Hey, that's a cinch!'

Sampei hustled back to the kitchen, but he couldn't find the tongs.

'Where are they? They were here just a second ago.'

He ran back to Mother, 'Mom, what if you don't have the tongs?'

'What if you don't have the tongs? Why, you look for them.'

'Zenta, Mom says we hunt for the tongs.'

They found the tongs and with them transferred an ember from the range to the charcoal stove. They laid charcoal on the ember and set the soup kettle back on the stove. And now . . . ?

Sampei hurried again to ask, 'Mom, we got the kettle on. Now what?'

'Put in the bonito flavoring, cut up some vegetables, and . . .'

'Got it!'

Sampei sprinted toward the kitchen even before she had finished speaking.

'Okay, Zenta, put in the flavoring. Then cut up some vegetables.'

'Vegetables? What kind of vegetables?'

'Gee, I missed that.'

Sampei flew back to his mother. 'Vegetables, Mom – which ones?'

'Green onions and potatoes.'

'Oh, green onions and potatoes, right?'

Off to the kitchen, Sampei announced, 'She says green onions and potatoes.'

'Onions and potatoes?' Zenta was puzzled. 'Where are they?'

'Whew!' – Cooking is certainly a tremendous amount of work.

Chapter Thirty-One

Just before noon, Zenta and Sampei heard the rumble of heavy wheels and flew out of the house. Outside their gate stood a horse and a large wagon. Next to them were Juzo Akazawa and the man from the court.

'Holy cats!'

Blood drained from their faces. Sampei knew he should go straight in and tell Mother, but that was out of the question. Kintaro and five or six other boys stood behind the wagon, their eyes on him. He couldn't retreat now.

He wanted to say, 'Hey, what do you think you're doing here?' But he didn't. He reined in his pounding heart and walked over to them with a calm face. For some reason, Kintaro's glare was somewhat softer than usual today. He was the first to speak.

'Sampei, how about playing?'

'Okay.'

Ginjiro, always the flatterer, came up close. 'Sampei,' he said, 'we're playing Olympics today.'

'Olympics, huh? I already played that the other day.' Sampei was one up on them.

'We're gonna triple jump.'

'So what?'

'And pole vault.'

'So?'

'And there's hurdles, too.'

'I know.'

'And how about the long jump?'

'I've done that lots of times.'

'Well, how about a tree-climbing race?'

'Hmmmm. Tree climbing, huh? The other day my big brother climbed up the persimmon tree one-handed!'

Ginjiro gasped, 'One-handed?'

'Right.'

'You're kidding.' Ginjiro couldn't accept that. He had to talk it over with the others.

'Say, Kin, how about climbing a tree one-handed? Nobody can do it, right?'

Kintaro didn't answer. The boys looked at each other, some tilting their heads in thought.

'Nobody can do it, right?'

Ginjiro went up to each boy, pumping his head boldly and repeating, 'Right?' He got their approval one by one as they shook their heads back at him.

'He can too!' Sampei objected loudly. He had to support his statement.

Kameichi stepped away from the group and sidled up to Sampei. 'Okay, you show us,' he said 'You climb the cedar in the shrine yard.'

'I'll show you I can do it.'

'Then show us right now.'

'Okay, I'll do it right now.'

Still glancing at each other, the boys started off toward the shrine. Sampei wondered if he had not gone too far. He looked back to check what Zenta was thinking. Zenta wasn't there. He had probably gone back into the house.

When Sampei turned to look he caught sight of Akazawa and the wagon driver hauling a chest of drawers from the house. 'Steady now, up we go.' They lifted it onto the wagon. This seemed a dark moment for Sampei's family, but he had already gone too far. He couldn't retreat now.

'Okay,' Sampei said, 'I'll climb it for you. Just bring it here and I'll climb it. Right now.'

The boys stopped in their tracks.

'I told you. He can't do it.'

'I can too. Okay, I'll go and show you.'

He set off. He had made up his mind to climb that cedar one-handed. No matter what.

Chapter Thirty-Two

After his boast, Sampei had to climb the cedar in the shrine compound, no matter what. He felt confident he could do it when Kameichi had dared him. Or rather was it only that he was determined to try?

He led the boys to the shrine. The closer he got the more his confidence crumbled. When he got to the tree he spit into both hands. The boys formed a circle around him and watched intently.

'This is just a try out,' he said, wrapping his arms round the tree. The trunk was as thick as a telephone pole.

'Hey ho, up we go!' He shinnied up some twelve feet before sliding smoothly down.

When he stood on the ground again he said, 'Okay, now's for real. With one hand, too. But if I make it what'll you guys do?'

They looked at each other. Not a boy had one thing to say.

'If I make it, will you guys climb it too?'

No one responded.

'Kin, how about you?'

'Not me. I never said I'd climb it.'

'Well, Gin, how 'bout you?'

'I never said it either.'

'Kameichi?'

'Same here.'

'So none of you guys'll climb it? Then nuts to it.'

Protests arose one after another:

'Why not?'

'You're chickening out.'

'You talked so big before.'

'Yeah,' Sampei replied, 'but this is the Olympics. One guy doesn't climb all by himself.'

Not one boy could refute that argument. They had to give in to his logic. Nevertheless, Kameichi and Tsurukichi mumbled under their breath, 'But you talked so big before.'

Sampei stood under the tree, his head turned back as he stared up at the trunk. He was racking his brains – wasn't there some way he could climb it one-handed?

A voice broke into his thoughts. 'Sampei!'

It was Zenta. He looked pale. He had been running and was out of breath. 'Mom says to come home.'

'Okay.'

In that instant, Sampei forgot all about climbing the tree. The brothers ran back home panting.

Sampei was stunned when he entered the house. For a moment he thought that it was already evening; the whole place looked gloomy. He looked around silently, walking from the entrance to the living room, from the living room to the back room. The rooms were empty. It looked like a vacant house. A small table, a broom and a duster were all that remained in the dining room.

He wanted more than anything to ask Mother what had happened. But he didn't have to. He knew. That man from the factory had come and taken everything away.

Mother was getting ready to go out. 'You boys stay here and watch the house,' she said, 'Mother's going to see the lawyer.' She went out biting her lip.

'Okay.'

She left the two boys in the middle of the dining room. They stood there for a long time. Neither was in the mood to sit down or stretch out on the floor. A house without furniture just didn't seem like home.

In fact, they didn't get the feeling that they were inside a house at all. They felt as though they were standing on the roadside, exposed to the wind and the rain.

Chapter Thirty-Three

Juzo Akazawa and the man from the court had taken away every last item that had been seized. They had said they were taking it to the factory for safekeeping. Akazawa figured that if they had left these items in the house, some of them might disappear or be hauled off somewhere.

Sampei's house now looked like nobody lived in it. It was dark. It was bleak. Zenta and Sampei stood in the midst of its emptiness looking dejected. Mother had gone to the lawyer's again and they didn't know what to do.

'Did they take the swing?' Sampei asked.

'Naw, they wouldn't take that.'

'Good. How about my tricycle?'

'Your trike? Well, maybe they did. I don't remember,' Zenta said as he shrugged his shoulders. Of course they had taken it.

'That's okay,' Sampei said. 'It was all beat up, anyhow.'

Their mood improved as they talked. They felt they needed to do something to raise their spirits.

'Let's play on the swing,' Sampei suggested.

Zenta quickly agreed. 'Let's go.'

They ran to the persimmon tree. Sampei got on first. Zenta pushed. After a half dozen turns they switched places. Zenta got on and Sampei pushed. They were too impatient to take such long turns, so they changed off, after each swing.

'Let's climb the persimmon tree.'

They raced to the top. The moment they reached their goal they were ready to slide down.

'Let's race down, okay? Reeeeady, Go!'

They plopped to the ground on their bottoms, skinning their knees on the way. It didn't bother them a bit. Not today. In fact, the hurt kept their minds off other matters.

'Let's race around the house now,' Zenta said.

'Great!'

'Ready, Set, Go! . . . No, wait. Hold it. Five times around,' Zenta added, 'Okay? Ending here at the persimmon tree. Got it? . . . Reeeeady, Go!'

They sprinted off. Zenta was of course the faster. Sampei was merely half way around, just passing the living room, by the time Zenta called out, 'Lap one.' And Zenta had already finished the second lap and had called out, 'Lap two,' when Sampei was only as far as the kitchen, just beginning his second lap.

Sampei figured he wouldn't have a chance at that rate, so he just skipped his second lap.

'Lap three, it's lap three,' he shouted at the top of his lungs.

As he started the final lap, Sampei kicked off his shoes, ran up on the porch, dashed through the back room and headed for the persimmon tree.

'Lap fiiiive,' he shouted.

With his short cuts, Sampei had almost managed to catch his brother. Of course Zenta protested.

'That's cheating, Sampei.'

'What do ya mean? You never said how to go around.'

'Cheater, cheater! You got another lap to go.'

Too exhausted to continue their quarrel, they stretched out on a mat lying under the persimmon tree. They were still gasping for breath, dripping wet and red as beets. Every scrape from climbing and sliding down the persimmon tree smarted. Still, it felt good to be so tuckered out.

They looked straight up at the sky and rested, putting everything out of their thoughts. After he had caught his breath, Sampei made a proposal.

'Zenta, how about ten laps next?'

'Ten laps?'

'Why not? Maybe even twenty!'

Sampei wanted to wear himself to a frazzle if possible. He had no way of helping his folks. Maybe that was the least he could do for them.

Noises at the gate brought them to their feet. It was Mother and Uncle Ukai. Their uncle, looking unusually glum, went into the house.

Chapter Thirty-Four

Mother told Sampei, right in front of Uncle Ukai, 'Now bow and tell your uncle you'll be a good boy. And ask him if he won't give you another chance to stay with him.'

Sampei stubbornly said, 'I don't want to.'

She got the same response every time, so she gave up.

The next day she took Sampei with her to town. She wanted to visit the clinic and ask the Director whether Sampei might walk the dog and feed the birds instead of Zenta.

The Director declined good-heartedly, 'Hmmm, well now, with a child this young, you know...'

They stopped at the park in town and sat down on a bench to rest before going home.

'Sampei, you know the Director said you wouldn't do for the chores at the clinic, don't you?'

'I know.'

'And you still won't go back to the Ukais'?'

'Nope.'

'But what am I to do then?'

Sampei had no answer. He turned various solutions over and over in his mind. 'Mom, if we go to the ocean, maybe we can find Robinson Crusoe's island.'

'There's no such place.'

'But Zenta said. He says there's goats and rabbits on it.'

Sampei imagined they could all go live there. His mother, however, had more important things on her mind. She ignored Sampei and became absorbed in her thoughts.

Finally she sighed and said dejectedly, 'Well, what shall I do?'

'Say, Mom, how about if me and Zenta sell newspapers?'

Sampei recalled having seen a boy selling papers when they passed the train station on their way to the clinic. His mother got up without answering and headed for the exit. Beyond the exit was a bridge spanning the wide river that flowed by the park.

She stopped when they got halfway across, leaned against the railing, and looked down into the water. She was still lost in thought. 'What if we threw ourselves in and drowned . . . ?'

After a while she looked up, her face wearing an uncommonly tender smile.

'Sampei.'

'Yeah . . .'

'What if Mother died?'

He was lost for an answer. Nor did he know if she was serious. He looked up into her face and smiled sweetly.

She brought her cheek close to his and asked, 'Well, what would you do?'

He could only continue to smile. Actually his mother's tenderness frightened him a bit.

'Sampei, if I died, you know you'd probably have to stay at the Ukais', don't you?'

She pressed her cheek hard against his. Her face seemed tinged with madness. Sampei kept on smiling. The bridge was virtually deserted and the sun was setting. Mother stopped talking and stared intently into the water.

Sampei then crawled up and straddled the railing. That was easier than standing – and more fun, too. It also gave him the idea of trying to imitate Uncle Ukai galloping along on his horse. Sampei lifted his hips, rocked his body, and joined his hands in front of him to hold the reins.

'Clippety-clop, clippety-clop.'

He squeezed his mouth to make the sound of galloping hooves and soon completely forgot about his mother standing next to him.

When she realized what he was doing, she suddenly embraced him and broke into sobs. 'Oh, Sampei!'

Then and there she made up her mind. No matter what happened, she would go on living. She would bring up Sampei.

Chapter Thirty-Five

Mrs Aoyama wept for a while, holding Sampei tightly while he straddled his horse on the railing. Then she wiped her tears away.

'Zenta's waiting. We'd better hurry back,' she said as she took Sampei's hand and hastened off.

'Mom, do you want me to go to the Ukais' or stay home?'

'I think you already know the answer.'

'Then I guess I'll go.'

'You'll go?'

'Yep, I'll go.'

She smiled through her tears when she heard him agree to go.

'Oh, Sampei, that's certainly a relief! But you won't get into mischief again, will you?'

'Nope. I won't climb any trees. I won't go to the river or the pond. I don't like rivers anyhow. I'll just stay in and read.'

'So you're going to be a good little boy?'

'Right. I'll greet Auntie as soon as I get there and tell her I won't get into any mischief. Then I'll study hard at school. I'll be first in class from the start. I'll be class monitor.'

'Really?'

'Really and truly. Then I'll go to middle school. And to college too. And when I finish college . . .'

At that point he was at a loss for words.

'After college, what then, Mom? Huh? What'll I be?' The question completely occupied his mind.

There was no need for his mother to fret about anything now. She'd be satisfied if only Sampei would return to the Ukais' – perhaps tomorrow – and if she could take Zenta to the clinic and start working.

'Zenta's waiting,' she said, trying to hasten their return. She felt so terribly relieved and lighthearted that she found herself quickening her pace every now and then. By the time she entered the gate she was in a very cheerful mood.

A glum Zenta welcomed them back.

Mother greeted him gently: 'Aren't you tired of waiting?'

'No.'

'Anybody come?'

'Nope.'

She was exhausted despite her cheerfulness, and sat down at the table in the dining room to catch her breath.

'I'll make your supper in a moment. You must be starved.'

Then she noticed the notebook lying in front of her. Zenta had been scribbling in the margins. When she picked it up, she discovered that it was an old diary. Her husband, using the notebook as a personal record, had crammed it with his small writing. The entries were dated 192–, which meant they had been written nine years earlier.

She was about to start reading when her eyes caught sight of something sandwiched between the pages. She opened the notebook and found a piece of official parchment paper. It had been folded twice. When she unfolded it she found writing on two sides. On one side was written:

Certificate of Transfer
This attests to the fact that Mitsuwa
Weaving transfers for the sum of ¥80,000
all its rights and obligations to the
Mitsuwa Weaving Company, Ltd.

Solemnly witnessed on this –th day of
the month of ______________ in the year of 192–
by

Ichiro Aoyama (seal)
Representative, Mitsuwa Weaving.

On the other side was the following:

Certificate of Receipt

This attests to the fact that the Mitsuwa
Weaving Company, Ltd., has acquired for
the sum of ¥80,000 all the rights and
obligations of Mitsuwa Weaving.

Solemnly witnessed on this –th day of
the month of ______________ in the year of 192–,
by

Bunzo Nagao (seal)
Director, Mitsuwa Weaving Co., Ltd.

Mrs Aoyama was pale when she finished reading. She sat back, thinking that these were surely the documents her husband had been accused of forging.

Chapter Thirty-Six

Until she checked the entry at the spot where the parchment paper had been inserted, Mrs Aoyama was not certain that these were indeed the forged documents her husband was accused of having used as evidence in a suit against his company,

The entry read:

> *Found the original. No need to use the forged documents I had Akazawa prepare. Can win the suit fair and square.*

Her hands trembled. Huge tears – defying efforts to blink them back – crowded the corners of her eyes. Then she laid her head on the table and buried her face in her sleeves. For a while she sobbed. When she raised her head, she found Zenta and Sampei sitting on either side and staring anxiously at her.

Her tear-streaked face greeted them with laughter.

'No need to worry now, boys! This is wonderful. You know, finding this paper makes everything all right. Daddy'll be able to come home, maybe even tomorrow.'

The news was too sudden for the boys. Unable to grasp the meaning of their mother's words, they just sat there wide-eyed and gaped at her. She wanted to explain the paper and what it meant, but she couldn't bear to waste another minute.

'All right, now, you two stay here and watch the house. Mother's going to the lawyer's again. I'll be right back. I might even come back with Daddy.'

There wasn't time for either of the boys to utter a word. Mother gathered up the diary and the document and hurtled into the night. She headed for town, trailed by the high-pitched sound of the closing gate.

Zenta and Sampei sat across from one another at the dining room table. For some time they couldn't utter a syllable. Over this brief ten-day period they had encountered a succession of drastic experiences. It seemed that an entire year had passed. The experiences flickered through their minds in dozens of scenes like a movie.

'Is Daddy coming home?' Sampei finally asked, almost as though mumbling to himself.

'That's what Mom said,' Zenta answered.

'When?'

'She said maybe tonight, maybe tomorrow.'

'Honest?'

The joy of having Father home again bubbled up in their hearts like water.

'I wonder if he really is,' Sampei said. 'Maybe tonight, maybe tomorrow morning, huh? When he comes, I'd better not be asleep. What'll I do, Zenta? Stay up all night?'

'Aw, he won't come back tonight.' Zenta often looked at the negative side of things.

'Why not?'

'He can't come back that fast.'

'Why not? He's at the police station in town, isn't he? He can walk home from there in no time.'

'Yeah, but the cops won't let him out that fast,' Zenta said.

'That's right. Maybe there's lots of cops around. They all have to talk it over. Even if one says, "Send Ichiro Aoyama home," another guy says, "Nothing doing." That's what he'll say. I hate cops who say that.'

Zenta found himself smiling at his brother.

Sampei continued, 'Zenta, when Daddy comes home, know what he'll say? He'll say, "My, Sampei, you've grown!" That's what he'll say. I'm positive.'

That seemed the right thing for Father to say.

Chapter Thirty-Seven

At last Father was coming home!

Mother had been cleaning the house since she got up. Uncle Ukai and the lawyer had gone to the police station to escort him back. And the boys? Mother suggested that they change their clothes and wait just beyond the factory for him. But the suggestion seemed somehow to embarrass them.

'Zenta, what should we do?'

After talking it over, they decided to make a new rising-sun flag and attach it to the tip of the persimmon tree. They would also cheer Dad with a *Hurrah!* from the treetop when he arrived. Once they had decided what to do, they were busy. Scurrying frantically, they turned up a bamboo pole and pasted together some sheets of writing paper to serve as a flag. Soon it was flapping in the breeze more splendidly than ever.

They climbed the tree immediately and practiced their *Hurrah!* while they waited. They shouted it in unison again and again, applauding after each cheer. Soon it was nine o'clock. Then it was ten.

'Dad won't be coming home any more today,' Zenta said. 'That's for sure.'

Even before he had finished the sentence, an automobile appeared from behind the factory – a shiny black, beetle-like car. It turned toward Sampei's house.

'Who's that? I wonder what's up?'

Neither imagined it was Daddy. The car stopped in front of their gate. Uncle Ukai got out; the lawyer got out; finally, a man with a sleepy face peppered with whiskers got out. He had on a rumpled summer kimono that looked as though he had been sleeping in it. It was Father. The three men went into the house without saying a word.

The boys wanted to shout their *Hurrah!* but this didn't seem the proper moment for cheers. They didn't even feel joyous as they stood motionless and dumb in the tree. Only their flag was moving. The silence was soon broken by gay laughter rising from the house. The grown-ups were apparently eating something to celebrate Dad's release. If it was a time for rejoicing, neither Zenta nor Sampei could remain silent for another minute. They wanted everyone to know they were there.

'Zenta, you shout *Hurrah!*'

'No, you do it.'

Sampei said it in a teeny voice.

Since neither had the nerve to bellow it out, they decided to play on the swing. They pushed each other hard enough to reach the sky. Father still didn't notice them. No sense swinging then, so they crept by the porch and hunched down directly outside the living room. They called out softly:

'Daddy!'

'Daddy!'

He didn't seem to hear them. They said it louder:

'DADDY!' ... and scampered off to hide behind the front door. After a while they crawled from behind the door and sneaked back by the porch.

'Daddy!' they called, and again ran off.

Their antics seemed to have no effect. The grown-ups went on talking in the living room. The boys heard voices mixed with peals of hearty laughter. Well, if they could not attract attention in the usual way, they thought, they'd just have to take some risks. Sampei would be the shock troops. He dashed out from by the porch, giving away his position. As he headed past the living room for the back door he yelled, 'Daaaaaady!'

Not to be outdone, Zenta followed the shock troops yelping, 'Daddy! Daddy! Daddy!' in three quick bursts as he charged past the living room. The boys met at the back door, so tickled with themselves that they hopped about and laughed joyously.

In the living room Mr Aoyama was telling his side of the incident:

I really took a beating from Akazawa. The rat had hidden the original contract, so I had to come up with a substitute. At the police station I told them that, while I had prepared it, I emphatically did not use the forged contract in the suit. Still, I had no way of proving that the document they showed me – which they claimed was the fake – was actually the genuine contract. I was in a real bind.

Chapter Thirty-Eight

Father had come home.

Akazawa and Sayama were taken to the police station. The authorities agreed that Akazawa had in fact hidden the genuine contract. Not only that, it turned out that the reason the court had attached the Aoyama's property had nothing to do with any debts which Sampei's father might have owed. Akazawa and Sayama claimed that the wages and bonuses Mr Aoyama had paid to the factory workers and office staff were excessive. The plan was to recover the factory's losses at Aoyama's expense.

The stockholders held another meeting while the police questioned Akazawa and Sayama. Kintaro's father was removed and Sampei's father became the Director again, as he had been before his arrest. The neighborhood boys once again gathered in front of the factory, pretending they were gatemen.

'Welcome, thanks for coming.'

'Number one, number two, number three.'

Sampei wasn't there. He was home playing on his swing. Tsurukichi and Kameichi huffed and puffed over to his house to tell him about the meeting.

'Sampei, we're already up to number sixteen. Hurry. C'mon over and call 'em out.'

'I don't feel like it. How about telling the guys to come over here instead? I'll tell you about the *kappa*. That's more fun. I went to Uncle Ukai's place, see, and rode the rapids in a tub. When I got to this real deep place, a huge turtle came floating up. What d'ya think was riding his back? Huh? A thing called a *kappa* with a dish on his head.'

When he heard about the *kappa*, Tsurukichi picked up a piece of tile lying on the ground and balanced it on his head.

'I'm the *kappa*. This is the huge turtle,' he said as he mounted

Kameichi, who was squatting beside him. 'Okay turtle, get going. Come on, let's get moving.'

With Tsurukichi on his back, Kameichi walked around on all fours making strange *ho-ho* sounds. Turtles don't make noises, but the effect wouldn't be quite right unless Kameichi made some sort of sound.

'Sampei, come on, get on,' Tsurukichi called out. 'This turtle is really neat. He rides nice, real nice.'

The three of them headed for the factory where all the boys ended up playing *kappa*. The turtles used a piece of rope for their tails. The *kappas* used a piece of tile for the plate on their heads.

Soon the boys were dissatisfied merely to crawl around. They chose up sides and raced between the factory gate and the office building. But the turtles, finding it difficult to race on all fours, stood up – their tails dangling – and carried the *kappas* piggy back. The rule was if a *kappa* dropped the plate, his team was out. The boys had a merry time. They completely forgot about the stockholders' meeting as they dashed back and forth in their strange race.

When Sampei's father reported back to work, the property which Akazawa had had seized and stored at the factory was hauled back to Sampei's house. Mr Aoyama had put in a good word for Akazawa and Sayama, and the police allowed them to return home.

Summer vacation was ending. It was nearly time for school to start. For the first time in many days a boy appeared at the Aoyama's gate.

'Sampei, come out and play,' he called.

Sampei flew out of the house.

It was Kintaro. 'Come on, Sampei, let's play,' he said.

'Okay, let's play.'

They walked off toward the factory, their arms around each other's shoulders. On the way they noticed Akazawa coming toward them. Although he was still fifty or sixty feet off, he was already smiling.

When he came up to them he looked straight at Sampei and said, 'Where are you going, sonny?'

Sampei didn't know what to say. Worse, he felt bad because Akazawa had completely switched his attitude and was ignoring Kintaro.

'I'm playing with Kin,' Sampei shot back loudly.

'My, you've got the spunk. Let's be friends, okay?'

'Forget it.'

Despite the rebuff, Akazawa was about to continue when Sampei cut him off: 'Kin, let's race.'

Kintaro, a good deal meeker than he was a week ago, fell in with Sampei's suggestion. The boys sped off.

After they had run a short way Sampei told Kintaro, 'I don't like that guy. He calls the cops for everything.'

Afterword

To the Reader

Someone once said that, aside from God, only a novelist can create people. Of course, the people a writer creates exist only on paper and in the imagination. But a good novelist creates characters who are 'believable' as people, who seem like real people to us as we read the story. Those are the characters we usually remember.

After reading this story about Sampei and Zenta Aoyama, you may want to ask whether you feel that the novelist, Jôji Tsubota (1890–1982), has created truly believable characters. Do these Japanese boys have feelings that differ from yours? Do you imagine that the things which made them feel happy or sad, angry or afraid, might also make you feel happy or sad, angry or afraid? Can you imagine being faced with the problems that faced the Aoyama family?

Children in the Wind first appeared as a serial in the *Asahi Newspaper*, in which it was published over a two-month period late in 1936. In Japan, quite a few novelists publish their stories first as serials in newspapers or magazines. The money is good, and the millions of subscribers to Japanese newspapers and magazines have a chance to read the story and get interested in it. If they find it interesting, readers will be anxious for the next installment. A serial also encourages the writer to bring current events into his tale. This gives the impression that one is actually living through the drama.

By the year 1936, Japan – like America – was starting to recover from the Great Depression. There were good reasons to be hopeful about domestic economic recovery and the expansion of trade with foreign countries.

But the year 1936 also marks the beginning of a gradual tightening of authoritarian controls throughout Japan. That was the year of political assassinations, the effective end of parliamentary government, and the rise of the militarists. From 1936 onward, militarist influence spread and intensified; not long afterward, the militarists had gained control of the entire educational system up to the university. In a sense, 1936 marks the beginning of the severely centralized authoritarian control of Japanese institutions that ended only with the nation's capitulation in August, 1945.

The Olympics were the biggest news during the late summer of 1936. By the time this story about the Aoyama family began running in the *Asahi*, Japanese athletes had already won several medals at the XIth Olympiad held in Berlin, Germany. The entire Japanese nation felt proud of these medalists. It is natural, therefore, that a story serialized in those days would mention the Olympics. Although *Children in the Wind* refers several times to the Olympics, it is not a story about sport. It is rather about serious things that happen to the Aoyama family. The chapters describe how the problems developed and how they were finally resolved.

We see the events unfold through the eyes of the brothers, Sampei and Zenta. One result of this way of writing the story is that – unless the author decides to tell us – we never completely understand the exact nature of the events that happen to these little boys. At the same time, this method forces us to feel very close to Sampei and Zenta. We see how two young boys try to express their deep feelings about the events that touch them. We view their involvement in these events. We understand how, because they stand on the edges of the adult world, they never clearly grasp what is happening to their family. They react by retreating into their own world of play and fantasy. Interestingly, the adults in the story do not seem to understand what is happening in the boys' world any better than the boys understand what is happening in the adults' world.

Many readers find it easy to become involved in this novel because the story is based on a true life experience. In 1929, several years before he began writing *Children in the Wind*, Tsubota was in Tokyo trying to make a living as a writer. His family asked him to return to his native village to help run the small factory they owned.

During the four years this task involved him, a bitter feud developed with a relative who wanted to gain control of the factory. The feud ended with the suicide of Tsubota's older brother, who had been the family head since 1898, when their father died. In the summer of 1933, terribly upset and shocked by his brother's death, Tsubota returned to Tokyo and began writing about his experience. Three years later, he produced this story about Sampei and Zenta.

Many believe it is his best work. Others think that it finally established him, at the age of forty-six, as a recognized writer of children's literature. Certainly this story shows how skilfully Tsubota could write a story from a child's point of view. That may account for the fact that *Children in the Wind* has appealed to several generations of Japanese children and adults alike.

Certain reasons for this appeal should be clear to the thoughtful reader. Tsubota's description of the Aoyama boys is both warm and realistic. We sympathize with them as storms in the adult world touch their lives. We appreciate the reasons why the boys roam back and forth between the realm of reality and the realm of imagination. It is easy to understand, therefore, why some say that Tsubota was the first Japanese writer to describe the world of children with convincing skill. No wonder his 'heroes' have had a lasting appeal in Japan, or that he wrote many other stories that feature these same Aoyama boys.

Sampei and Zenta have feelings and thoughts that should certainly seem familiar. At the same time, however, some elements in the story you may not recognize or find easy to grasp. After all, these events took place long ago in a distant foreign land with customs quite different from ours.

For example, when Japanese in *Children in the Wind* sit down, do not imagine that they are using a chair. Most houses in those days did not have flooring, but thick mats called *tatami*. People sat directly on the *tatami*, often using a cushion. It is impossible to mop or wipe the dirt off *tatami*, so of course outdoor shoes must be left at the entrance. At school or in the office, Japanese sit at a desk, the way we do. But they wear special indoor footwear to keep the floors clean. Children who have been playing outdoors have to remember to wash their feet and legs before going back into the classroom or the house.

Once inside the home, we find many differences. One very important difference is that Sampei, Zenta, and their mother all sleep together in the same room. That room is not set aside especially as a bedroom either, but may serve, during the daytime, as the living room. At night, Mother simply pushes aside the little dining table and cushions, takes the mattresses, covers, and bedclothes from the closet, and lays them on the *tatami* mats. In summertime, the entire family usually sleeps inside a single, room-sized mosquito net. That explains why Sampei's mother awoke so quickly when he got out of bed in the middle of the night.

Clothing in those days was quite a bit different from what you might imagine. Before 1945, Japanese woman – particularly in rural areas like the one where the Aoyamas lived – wore kimono all year round. Then, as now, most men wore suits to work, but they changed into more comfortable Japanese clothing the moment they returned home. Children wore kimono much more often than they do today. In the summer, however, boys dressed generally the way anyone you know might dress on hot and humid days. Boys tended to wear short pants up through about the age of twelve, and they had to wear uniforms to school. Sometimes they even wore their uniform caps during vacation time.

In 1936, compulsory free education in Japan consisted of the six grades of elementary school. Both boys and girls had to attend, starting at age six. Of course, the State had exclusive control of elementary education. The only kindergartens that existed in those days were run by missions or other private institutions.

Because secondary education – which meant middle school – was not compulsory, it required both tuition and entrance examinations. That, of course, meant that education beyond elementary school was restricted to people of some substance. In a predominantly agricultural milieu, where workers on the farm were always in demand, most of the Japanese people had minimal opportunity for (or interest in) continuing the education of their children. When average people decided to invest in further schooling, it was usually a son whom they decided to support.

Rural Japanese in those days rarely addressed their aunts and uncles by their given names. That is, they did not usually say 'Aunt Sue' or 'Uncle Jim' but rather, 'Aunt Jones' or 'Uncle Smith.' We do not know the given names of Sampei's uncle and aunt, so in the translation I simply follow the Japanese custom. Moreover, Sampei seldom addresses his older brother by his given name. He uses instead a term that means 'older brother'.

In this case, it was easier and far more natural to follow normal English usage.

Tsubota Jôji [Japanese order: Tsubota is the family name] (1890–1982) was born and raised in Ishii, a small village in Okayama Prefecture. His family ran a midget factory that produced wicks for lamps and candles; it is this factory that appears – quite anonymously – in *Children in the Wind* and many other Tsubota stories. After graduating in 1907 from Kanagawa Middle School, run by Okayama Prefecture, Tsubota aspired to enter Waseda University in Tokyo. Waseda, famous at that time for training journalists and writers, was the obvious choice of a young man who thought of becoming a writer. After dropping out of school several times, once to serve a year in the military, he finally graduated in 1915. He wrote his graduation thesis on Lafcadio Hearn. For some years after graduation he spent his time translating works from English into Japanese, working in the Waseda library, helping run the family's wick factory in Ishii, and editing coterie magazines in which he could publish his works.

In the spring of 1923 he finally decided that he would devote himself exclusively to literature; his activities as a writer of children's literature began in earnest when he was already thirty-three years of age. He used his three sons as models for many works now recognized as among the most effective descriptions of children in Japanese literature.

I would like to thank the many people whose helpful criticisms and suggestions have improved my translation. Most must go unnamed, but I cannot neglect to mention particularly Professors Ben Befu and Iida Gakuji, as well as Marian Malotky and Marilyn Kurth. I also want to thank Professor Howard Hibbett of Harvard University, and Mr Milton Rosenthal, formerly of Unesco (Paris), for first suggesting that I translate *Children in the Wind*.

Van Nuys, California   ROBERT EPP

For Product Safety Concerns and Information please contact our EU
representative GPSR@taylorandfrancis.com
Taylor & Francis Verlag GmbH, Kaufingerstraße 24, 80331 München, Germany